BLOOD
ON THE
BEACH

SARAH N. HARVEY AND ROBIN STEVENSON

BLOOD ON THE BEACH

ORCA BOOK PUBLISHERS

Library and Archives Canada Cataloguing in Publication

Harvey, Sarah N., 1950–, author
Blood on the beach / Sarah N. Harvey and Robin Stevenson.

Issued in print and electronic formats.
ISBN 978-1-4598-1293-2 (paperback).—ISBN 978-1-4598-1294-9 (pdf).—
ISBN 978-1-4598-1295-6 (epub)

I. Stevenson, Robin, 1968–, author II. Title.
PS8615.A764B56 2017   C813'.6   C2016-904526-9
                          C2016-904527-7

First published in the United States, 2017
Library of Congress Control Number: 2016949056

Summary: In this thriller for young adults, eight teens spend a scary week on a remote island.

Orca Book Publishers is dedicated to preserving the environment and has printed this book on Forest Stewardship Council® certified paper.

Orca Book Publishers gratefully acknowledges the support for its publishing programs provided by the following agencies: the Government of Canada through the Canada Book Fund and the Canada Council for the Arts, and the Province of British Columbia through the BC Arts Council and the Book Publishing Tax Credit.

Cover design by Teresa Bubela
Cover image by Getty Images

ORCA BOOK PUBLISHERS
www.orcabook.com

Printed and bound in Canada.

20 19 18 17 • 4 3 2 1

To mystery lovers of all ages.

SATURDAY

ONE

Caleb

"Let me guess," I yelled. "First time on a Zodiac?"

The girl hanging over the side of the boat looked up at me and grimaced, her face as gray-green as the waves. Round cheeks, streaked with mascara and snot. Smeared dark lipstick. Bloodshot brown eyes. The rest of her was covered in the orange flotation suit we'd all had to put on for the hour-long trip to the island. Fifteen minutes in and she was a goner.

"Sorry," she mumbled. I could barely hear her over the roar of the engine. "Not good with boats."

"No shit," I said. "Word of advice—check which way the wind is blowing next time you hurl. Blowback is a bitch."

She groaned and retched again. I moved away from her, distancing myself from the possibility of flying puke.

Ordinarily I liked being out on the water. Not that day. It was the first day of a week-long sentence, not just for me but for the other seven misfits on the Zodiac. Four girls and three guys—and me. Stuck on a remote island for a week with three adults, one of whom was on the Zodiac with us—though not, I noticed, wearing an orange suit. His name was Warren, and he was an ex-cop, not a counselor. He had told us he was going to be our boot-camp guy, responsible for, as he put it, *pushing us beyond our perceived limits.*

Warren had a shaved head, a lot of tatts (one of them said *Sweat + Sacrifice = Success*) and really impressive biceps. I figured that was why he was wearing the muscle shirt despite the cold wind. I'd already seen some of the girls checking him out, although he had to be at least thirty-five. He and his wife, Claire, ran INTRO, In Nature to Renew Ourselves, a program for "at-risk" teens. I hadn't met Claire yet, but according to the INTRO brochure she had a PhD in psychology: *Doctor* Claire Addison. She and another counselor were already on the island, waiting for us. There was an older guy on the boat too, standing next to Warren. He was at least fifty, dressed in filthy jeans, a grubby gray T-shirt and a battered ballcap that read *Smile if you're not wearing underwear.* His purpose on the boat seemed to be limited to driving, smoking and leering at the girls. No way was he an INTRO counselor.

One of the girls, a tiny blond with glasses and a way-too-big flotation suit, staggered forward from where she had been sitting. I think she was trying to get away from the puker too, but Zodiacs aren't exactly a smooth ride, especially when there's chop. It didn't help that we were going pretty fast. Everybody except me, the puker and now this girl was huddled on the benches, not speaking, even when Warren yelled, "Isn't this great, kids?" as the Zodiac slammed into another wave.

The blond girl lost her balance and stumbled right into me. I grabbed on to her, and she stiffened, pulling away from me before she'd even regained her footing.

"Well, this sucks," she said.

"Which part?"

She gave me a sideways look. "All of it. The boat, the boot-camp guy, INTRO—the whole thing. It's bullshit." She scowled at me as if I was the one who had signed her up, then glanced over at the puker. "At least I'm not doing *that*," she said. "I wouldn't have thought Imogen would be the one to lose her lunch."

When I lifted an eyebrow, the blond girl said, "She seems pretty tough. At least, from what she told me on the bus coming up here. I can tell you where all her piercings are, if you like."

It was my turn to grimace. "No thanks," I said. Warren had given us strict instructions not to ask our fellow prisoners what crime they were in for—some crap about respecting personal boundaries—but I couldn't help wondering why she had been sent to INTRO, since she hardly looked like an "at-risk" teen. More like your average suburban high school girl, someone whose biggest problem is not being good at math.

"I'm Caleb," I said.

"Alice." She narrowed her eyes. "You look like a rugby player."

It didn't sound like a compliment.

I nodded. "Rugby, soccer, basketball, baseball."

"What? No tennis? No golf?"

What was her problem? "Who can afford that? What about you?" She didn't look athletic, not even in a tiny-gymnast way. More nerdy, really. A miniature nerd with a bad attitude.

"Team sports?" She shook her head. "I peaked in second grade, when my friend Janna and I won the three-legged race. It was all downhill from there."

I laughed despite my irritation. "What about the other inmates? Know anything about them?"

She nodded. "Imogen's met one of the guys before—Jason, the short guy with curly hair. Apparently he got caught 'in the commission of a B and E.' First offense, so this is his best option. The rest of them—no idea. What about you? What are you in for?"

She looked up at me, her eyes obscured by the salt spray on her glasses and the hair whipping across her face.

"Didn't you hear what Warren said?" I asked. "Boundaries."

"Oh, so we can talk about everyone else, just not you?"

I shrugged.

"Boundaries," she said dismissively. "Like that's gonna last. By the end of tomorrow, we'll know all about each other. For sure. What stupid crimes we're supposed to have committed, why we've been sent here."

I shrugged again, and she continued. "So let's at least make this boat ride interesting. What do you think he's in for?" She pointed at a guy sitting near the bow of the boat. The girl sitting next to him was obviously trying to ignore him, even when he yelled, "Whale!" Everybody else leaped up off their benches, raced over to one side of the boat and peered where he was pointing. The Zodiac hit a bigger-than-average wave, and one of the girls had to grab a rope to keep from being tossed overboard.

"Sit down!" Warren bellowed. "That was a log, not a whale! Endangering your fellow campers is not a good start to the trip, Chad. We'll talk about this later."

Chad smirked and said, "Looked like a whale to me" before he sat down, brushing his long stringy hair out of his eyes. The girl next to him got up and moved to another bench, and Alice asked, "So what do you think? Drugs, alcohol, assault, vandalism, grand theft auto, resisting arrest, reckless endangerment?"

I thought for a minute. "Is stupidity a crime?"

Alice laughed. "It should be, but there's no island big enough for all the stupid people." She nodded in Chad's direction. "I bet he's a dealer. Low level. Weed. Got caught selling to middle-schoolers."

I looked over at Chad again. "Seems about right. Chronic stoner. Thinks he's smarter than he is."

"You pick someone," Alice said. "What about her?" She jerked her head toward the girl who had moved away from Chad. She was tall and very thin, with long dark hair streaked with blue. I could only see her profile—large beaky nose, downturned mouth, pale skin with a strawberry birthmark on her jawline.

"Doesn't look like the criminal type. I'll go with depressed and suicidal with a side of anxiety." The minute I said it, I felt bad. The girl looked lonely and sad, which was probably appropriate under the circumstances. I felt a bit that way myself.

"And that guy, the one in the red tuque?" Alice said. "I think he runs a brothel out of his parents' basement, catering to teen guys who can't get laid. He got caught when he tried to pimp out his little sister to her school principal's son."

"Where do you come up with this stuff?" I said. The tuque guy looked like a regular guy to me. Good-looking, I guess, in a boy-band kind of way, but definitely not a criminal mastermind.

"Overactive imagination," Alice said. "And my mom's a cop, so I hear a lot. You wouldn't believe some of the stuff she has to deal with."

I didn't like cops. They never helped my mom after Barry used her as a punching bag. And they came down on me hard when I finally stepped up and turned the tables on the prick. Like I didn't have any reason to beat the crap out of him after all the times he hit my mom. But the way the cops (and Barry) saw it, I was a danger—not just to Barry, but to society. They kept me locked up for two days because Mom was too busy tending to Barry's broken nose and his fractured arm to come and bail me out.

When she finally did, she would barely speak to me. And then she made this deal with the cops—it was called diversion—because it was my first offense: I could go to INTRO rather than enter the justice system and maybe end up with a record. Like Alice, I thought the whole INTRO thing was bullshit, including the name. As acronyms go, it was pretty pathetic.

"Time for one more," Alice said, nudging me with her elbow and nodding toward a girl who was trying to get cozy with Warren. Even from a distance I could see that she was wearing heavy eyeliner, false eyelashes and bright-pink lip gloss. Her gigantic hoop earrings flashed in the sun as she threw her head back and laughed at something Warren was saying. Her hair was long and shiny and an unlikely shade of red—somewhere between candy apple and pumpkin. It clashed with her flotation suit, which she had unzipped partway to reveal some impressive cleavage.

"One of Mr. Tuque's girls?" I said. "Or maybe an underage drag queen?"

"Or both," Alice said. "I can't wait to find out!" She turned to me. "So that leaves you. And me. Let me guess. You got caught selling steroids to your teammates on the football team. Or maybe you had a bad case of 'roid rage and attacked a referee."

I'm used to people thinking I'm a big dumb jock. I mean, that's what I look like, but I had hoped Alice was smarter than that. Turned out she was just like everyone else.

"Yeah, you got me," I said. "So what's your deal? Since we're judging by appearances, I'd have to say anorexic. Or possibly alcoholic. Which is it?"

"At least I'm not brain-damaged from too many concussions," Alice snapped. "Asshole." And with that she lurched off to join Imogen, who had finally stopped puking and was hunched miserably on a bench. They turned their backs on me, leaving me to enjoy the scenery, which now included a solitary island—spiky green trees, rocky shore, a small dock with a flagpole. Red letters on a yellow flag spelled INTRO. Warren yelled, "Land ho!" as we neared the dock, in case we hadn't figured out this was our destination.

As we came closer I could see two figures on the dock. One was a short curvy brunette in tight jeans, a red-and-yellow INTRO T-shirt and gigantic movie-star sunglasses. The other was a slight, balding dude with wire-rimmed glasses. All his clothes looked brand-new—Gore-Tex jacket, khaki cargo pants, Keen sandals with thick gray socks. Pretty sure the great outdoors wasn't his natural habitat. He almost fell off the dock trying to help Warren and the old guy secure the Zodiac.

"Take off your flotation suits and then go and introduce yourselves to Claire and Rahim," Warren said. "And don't forget your stuff. Anything left behind becomes Del's property."

The guy in the stupid ballcap—Del, obviously—added, "So if you don't want me wearing your boxers or bras, don't leave 'em behind!"

"His Zodiac, his rules," Warren said, laughing. He punched Del in the shoulder. "Del's a local up in these parts. He takes all our campers to and from the island. Been doing it since we started. Our freezer at the camp? Chock full of crab and shrimp he's caught. You guys behave yourselves, maybe we'll have a seafood feast one of these nights."

Warren clapped all the guys on the back as we staggered off the boat. He kept his hands off the girls, I noticed, although the girl with the big earrings asked him to help her onto the dock. He refused. "First step in your therapy— rely on yourself. You can do whatever you set your mind to, Mandy."

Mandy glared at him and stumbled off the boat, dragging a gigantic purple duffel bag behind her. I heard her mutter, "Screw you" as she staggered up the dock toward Claire and Rahim. Once we were all on dry land, Del fired up the Zodiac and took off, yelling, "See ya in a week, losers!"

Definitely not counselor material.

TWO
Caleb

I'd only ever seen receiving lines in movies, but that's what it was like on the dock—after we shed our survival suits, we lined up to shake hands, first with Claire, then with Rahim, as if they were royalty and we were their humble servants. Claire was young—late-twenties maybe—and attractive. Her handshake was brisk and dry; she looked each of us in the eye, repeated our names and told us to call her Claire. Rahim used two soft, damp hands to clasp each camper's hand. He was young-ish too—under thirty, I guessed, despite the receding hairline. "You can talk to me about anything," he murmured as we passed by. Or "I'm so glad to share your journey with you." I didn't know what to say—I wasn't planning to talk to him about anything—so I just said, "Thanks, man," and moved up the little ramp to the island.

Above the dock was a narrow path leading to an open grassy area. In the clearing stood a rustic wooden building.

Paths led into the woods, where I could see three smaller cabins and a couple of dilapitated sheds. A rocky beach was on my right—a slope of gray pebbles, strewn with driftwood, the long, smooth logs bleached white as bones. Two kayaks—one yellow, one red, the only splashes of color—were pulled up on the beach, above the high-tide line.

Warren bounded ahead of the group and announced, "See this path?" He stamped one heavy-booted foot against the hard-packed dirt. "We're going to clear one just like it all the way to the other side of the island! The first step toward finding balance is to connect with your physical self. I'm gonna push you pretty hard. But you know what they say: *Pain is just weakness leaving your body!* Now follow me." He grinned and charged up the path. We straggled behind like ducklings, with Claire and Rahim herding us along. I considered grabbing a kayak and making a run for it—a paddle for it, really—but I knew I wouldn't get far.

"On your far right is the girls' dorm," Warren said as we neared the clearing. "Far left is the guys'. And that's the way it stays." He stopped suddenly and turned to face us. "Am I clear?"

We murmured our assent (although I thought I heard Chad snort and mutter, "As if"), and Warren continued with the guided tour. "Staff cabin next to the guys' cabin, mess hall next to the girls'. We're off the grid here—solar power, composting toilets, limited water supply, so no long showers, people. Not that you'll want to, since there's no hot water in your cabins. Only in the kitchen."

He laughed, and Claire took over. "Why don't you go and drop off your gear and meet us at the mess hall in fifteen minutes for an orientation session?"

As we plodded off to our cabins, all I could think was, Please God, no bunk beds. Chad was right behind me as I opened the door. "Dibs on this one," he said, pushing past me and throwing himself on the bed nearest the door.

The windows were small and high, making the interior of the cabin unnecessarily dark. I squinted into the gloom, waiting for my eyes to adjust. There were four beds, each one made up with gray blankets bearing the red-and-yellow INTRO logo. I chose the bed farthest from Chad's, although it wasn't far enough. The whole cabin smelled dank and sour, and the air felt too still. I sat down on the edge of my bed and wondered how many other people had slept in it.

The curly-haired guy tossed his bag on the bed next to mine. "I'm Jason," he said, extending his hand. "Breaking and entering. Extenuating circumstances. You?"

He had a trace of an accent—Scottish or Irish maybe. "Caleb," I replied. "Assault. Abusive stepdad."

"Cool." He stuck his thumbs through his belt loops and jerked his chin toward Chad, who appeared to have fallen asleep as soon as his head hit the pillow. "That's Chad. He sold some weed to a cop. He's a few fries short of a Happy Meal."

"I heard that, dude," Chad mumbled. "Makes me hungry."

The final addition to our cabin was Tuque Guy. He stumbled into the room, pulling a wheeled blue suitcase behind him. We watched him in silence as he parked his suitcase next to the only remaining empty bed and said, "I'm Nick. And this…well, it's not exactly the Ritz, is it? I think I could *renew* myself"—he made air quotes with his fingers—"more effectively if there was, like, a gym. And a TV. And…well. Just saying."

He gestured at the roughhewn cedar walls, the burlap curtains, the thrift-shop lamps. I laughed, and we introduced ourselves.

"What are you in for, Nick?" Jason asked.

"Oh, you know. This and that." Nick rolled his eyes. "My parents want to, you know, toughen me up. So here I am. Ready to lock and load. Rock and roll. Whatever."

"You guys got any food?" Chad sat up and yawned.

"Nope," Jason said. "Try the mess hall."

"Dude, I have no idea what that is," Chad said, absently scratching his balls. I had a feeling Chad did a lot of things absently.

Nick sighed. "Haven't you ever seen *Star Trek*? It's where you go to eat."

"What?" Chad said. "There are mess halls on *Star Trek*?"

"It's next to the girls' cabin," Jason said. "There's food."

"Girls and food. Two of my favorite things." Chad stood up and strolled out the door.

Nick and Jason and I followed him after a few minutes. The door to the staff cabin was shut when we walked by, and I wondered if Warren and Claire and Rahim all shared one room, like we did. Awkward. There was a collection of shells on the steps, but otherwise it looked like our cabin: wilderness institutional and run-down. The mess-hall doors were wide open, and the girls and Chad were gathered around one of the dark wooden tables, eating what turned out to be cut-up fruit (the apples were already turning brown) and some kind of healthy cookie that probably tasted like sweetened cardboard. Jugs of juice sat next to an assortment of mismatched mugs. I felt like I was in preschool again.

Claire clapped her hands at the front of the room. "Choose a mug. It'll be yours for the week. Keep it clean and don't lose it."

I grabbed a blue mug that said *Every day is a second chance.*

"This blows," said Chad, picking up a purple mug and reading out, "*Trust yourself. You know more than you think you do.* What does that even mean?"

I looked over at Alice, who was trying to choose between a white mug (*When opportunity doesn't knock, build a door*) and a green one (*Every accomplishment starts with the decision to try*). I could think of a few slogans that'd suit her better.

By the time we all had our mugs (Nick and Imogen almost came to blows over an orange one that said *Go the extra mile*), Warren and Rahim had joined Claire. She clapped her hands again, and Warren boomed, "Sit down, people. Orientation starts now. And enjoy those afternoon snacks—they're the last food we're going to prepare for you!"

Claire held up a large piece of paper. "This is the kitchen roster. Breakfast is served at seven, lunch is at noon, dinner at five. You will work in teams of two. Be prepared to be in the kitchen"—she gestured to the far end of the mess hall—"at least one hour before serving time. Menus have been set already. None of the food is complicated. All you have to do is work together and serve your fellow campers and the three of us."

"And don't forget the cleanup, Claire," Warren added. "Leave the kitchen spick-and-span for the next guys."

"Are you freakin' kidding me?" Jason said in my ear.

Before I could reply, Rahim said, "I know it sounds like a lot, but kitchen duty can be fun. You get a chance to make a new friend, and you have the satisfaction of providing nourishment for the other campers. Sound good?"

A few people groaned, and Claire clapped her hands again. "Time to pair up," she said. "Line your mugs up on the table so they make a rainbow. White mug on the left, black on the right."

The tall girl (she had a black mug with the words *Know thyself* on it) put her mug down on the table and said, "White, red, orange, yellow, green, blue, purple, black." Her voice was soft, almost a whisper—as if she was too timid to take up any space in the world. My mom was like that, but in her case I knew why—Barry. We arranged the mugs in the correct order, and then Claire said, "Red and white, orange and yellow, green and blue, purple and black. Grab your mugs and say hello to your co-chefs, everybody."

THREE
Alice

I glanced down at the green mug in my hand.

"Looks like we're stuck with each other," a low voice said behind me.

I turned. It was the dumb jock from the Zodiac. Great. "Yeah, us *anorexics* make fabulous chefs."

"Um, *'roid rage*? Remember?"

Like a whiny little kid. *Mom, she started it.* I didn't bother responding.

"Look, can we start over?" He put his mug beside mine. "I'm Caleb. In case you forgot. And we are…green and blue. Very…uh…nature."

"Very nature?" I raised an eyebrow. "So outdoors. Much wow."

He laughed—he had a rather nice laugh, actually—and held out a hand. "Come on. Friends?"

"Well, co-chefs anyway." I shook his hand. "And I am not *very nature*. City kid, all the way. Trees are not my thing. Wilderness is not my thing. Solar power is fine as an eco-friendly backup to the real thing, but cold showers and no Wi-Fi? Yeah. Not my thing."

"So what is your thing?" he asked.

"You mean, why am I here? Among the *very nature* trees instead of in my high-rise condo with my couch, TV and PlayStation?"

"Yeah. If you want."

He was good-looking, I guess, if you were into square jaws and muscles. Which I was not. He also had dark skin, darker eyes and ridiculous eyelashes. Mandy was going to be all over him. "My mother worries too much," I said. "That's why I'm here."

"Your mother the cop?"

"Yeah. She also has an overactive imagination. Family trait." I looked away from him, glanced around at the other campers. "Uh, are we supposed to be doing anything in particular?"

"Aha. A rule follower," Caleb said. "Interesting."

I scowled at him. "I just wondered if there was a point to this conversation."

Claire clapped her hands. "Okay! Everyone's met their partners. Now we're all going to get to know each other, so grab a chair and let's make a circle over here." Another clap. "Circle time!"

Circle time. The previous summer I had worked at a karate camp for six- to ten-year-olds—Little Dragons, it was called—and this felt a lot like that. I hoped Claire wasn't going to make us play Duck, Duck, Goose.

With much nails-on-chalkboard screeching, we dragged our heavy wooden chairs into a circle and sat there, checking each other out while pretending not to give a shit. Druggies, dealers, delinquents. I tried to think of a collective noun for my new peer group. A rabble of felons. A scourge of liars. A plague of losers.

I still couldn't believe my mother had done this to me. Every time I thought about it, an awful rage surged up inside me, and I wanted to throw things or hit someone. My mother and I had always been super close—it had been just the two of us since I was a baby. But right now—really, ever since she'd told me she was sending me to INTRO—I almost hated her.

"I know you're probably all tired," Claire said. Her voice was sugar-filled, over-the-top perky, a little too high-pitched. Phony, I thought. It was a weird thing I'd noticed before—a lot of adults who worked with teens were phony. My school was full of them. Sometimes I wondered if they were only phony when they were around teens and turned into real people after work.

"Most of you have had long journeys," she went on, "traveling to our little island from Vancouver, and Imogen, I heard you were a bit seasick on the boat…"

Imogen ignored her. She pulled an enormous purse from under her chair and began rummaging through it.

I'd never carried a purse, and I always wondered what other girls kept in them. Wallet, phone, keys, tampons? You didn't need a bag the size of a microwave oven for that.

"Feeling all right now?" Claire asked. Like it wasn't totally obvious that the last thing Imogen wanted was to have extra attention drawn to her puking.

Ignoring Claire, Imogen reapplied a slick coat of blood-red lipstick. Perfectly, without a mirror. I don't do makeup—it makes me look like a little kid who got into her mom's cosmetics bag—but I had to admit, there was something impressive about it.

I'd spent most of the bus ride listening to her tell one exaggerated story after another. At least, I hoped for her sake they were exaggerated, because to be honest, some of them were more than a bit shocking. I'd tried to act cool, but I could practically feel my eyes getting bigger and rounder the longer she talked. And I'm a cop's kid, so it's not like I'm a total innocent.

"Well," Claire said. "Let's have a quick round of introductions, and then we'll give you some time to unpack and settle in before we start on the afternoon's activities. How about we go first, Warren? Rahim?"

"Great idea, Claire," Rahim said. He sounded excessively enthusiastic, like he was her co-host on a talk show. *The Claire and Rahim Show*. I wondered how Warren felt about that.

As if he'd read my mind, Warren jumped in. "Works for me. Why don't you start us off, Claire?"

Claire clapped her hands again—god, was she going to keep doing that all week?—and flashed her big white teeth at us. *The better to eat you with, my dear.* There was definitely something creepy about her. All that smiling, but I felt like she was playing a part. The approachable counselor, professional but warm and friendly. I didn't trust her in the least. For that matter, I didn't trust any of them—not her or Warren or Rahim or any of my fellow inmates. This whole place was creeping me out.

"Now, I don't want you to disclose anything too personal yet," Claire said. "There'll be plenty of time for that in group, after we've talked about confidentiality and established some basic ground rules. This is simply a fun get-to-know-your-fellow-campers warm-up, okay?"

Rolled eyes all around.

"So here's what I want you to share. Your name. And three things about yourself. Two truths—and a lie. And then everyone will guess which one is the lie. Got it?"

Seriously? Two truths and a lie was the oldest icebreaker around. Still, it could be worse. I remembered some of the exercises we did with the kids at karate camp and felt grateful that Claire wasn't forcing us to make a human knot or play Charades.

"Oh, fun!" Rahim said.

I made a face. Caleb caught me, I guess, because he winked, and to my annoyance, I found my cheeks heating up. Ugh, what was *that* about?

"So I'll start. My name is Claire. I'm married to Warren, I love cats, and I'm allergic to celery."

"No one's allergic to celery," Chad blurted out. "Like, I don't think celery is even an allergy."

"No shit," Imogen said. "It's a vegetable."

I laughed out loud. Imogen might have her problems, but she was also hilarious. So totally deadpan.

He stared at her like he had no idea what she meant. After a pause, he shrugged. "Yeah, I guess. I don't really eat vegetables."

"Come on, people." Rahim looked around the circle. "What do the rest of you think?"

"We already know she's married to Warren," the tall skinny girl said, twisting her long hair in her fingers. "It's in the brochure."

"Doesn't mean it's true," Mandy pointed out. "Could be they just thought that'd be good for the business. Maybe they're not actually a couple at all."

Imogen snorted. "Yeah, you wish."

Warren ran both hands over his bald head. "We're married. Been married for six years."

I actually happened to know this was true. Mom didn't know him super well or anything, but their paths had crossed a bunch of times before he met Claire and left the police force to start INTRO. That was part of the reason my mom had sent me here—she said he'd always seemed like a good guy.

"She doesn't like cats," Jason said, sounding bored. "That's the lie." He leaned back in his chair, letting his knees fall apart and totally manspreading.

"You're right," Claire said. "But only because I'm horribly allergic to them. *And* to celery. Which is a shame, since I'm a vegan." She smiled, scanning the circle. "Okay. So you see how this works?"

A few nods and some more eye rolls. A yawn from Chad.

"Rahim, why don't you go next?" Claire suggested.

The exercise dragged on painfully. We learned that Rahim had a master's degree in social work and was diabetic; that Warren played football and had his appendix out last year; that Imogen had sixteen piercings and a tattoo of a tiger on her thigh; and that Tara—the tall skinny timid girl with the heart-shaped birthmark on her cheek—had almost drowned as a child and was terrified of water. Jason lied about being a marathon runner but told us that his dad was Irish, which explained his accent: apparently his family had moved back to Belfast for most of Jason's childhood to avoid some bookie who wanted repayment on his father's gambling debts. Jason's hero was an outlaw called William Brennan, who sounded like an Irish version of Robin Hood, stealing from the rich to give to the poor and all that. Nick played violin and spent a lot of time looking after his eight-year-old cousin, and Chad seemed to miss the point of the game completely and made up a bunch of stupid stuff. Mandy liked clothes and hated math. And Caleb stuck to the sports-related facts he'd already shared on the Zodiac—rugby, soccer, *blah, blah, blah.*

Then it was my turn. "I'm Alice," I began and cleared my throat. I'm not shy, but I really would prefer never to have to speak in groups. "I play *Call of Duty*, I have a black belt in karate, and I'm addicted to *CSI*."

Caleb laughed. "Okay, well, that's easy. You're definitely not the karate kid."

There were murmurs of agreement. I turned to face him. "Why would you assume that, Caleb? Because I'm a girl?"

"Because you're, like, tiny? I don't know. You just don't look the type." His eyes narrowed. "Are you? Seriously? Because that would be pretty cool."

"And I *hate* first-person shooters," I said.

"You said something about your TV and your PlayStation." He sounded defensive. "So I figured…"

"FPS games are for people who don't have the brains for strategy games or the skill for platformers."

"Dude, I play *Call of Duty*," Chad cut in. "And *Battlefield*. And *Planetside 2*."

"Right. Thanks for making my point for me," I snapped.

Rahim cleared his throat. "Alice. It sounds like you are upset. Hurt, perhaps, and angry. Do you want to talk about that?"

I shook my head. "Yeah, no." I didn't want to talk about anything at all. Not to Rahim. Not to anyone. A week of this crap stretched out ahead—a whole goddamn week. It had only been an hour, and I was already losing my mind.

FOUR
Alice

Eventually the torture session ended and we were set free to unpack our stuff into the small dressers at the ends of our beds. Rahim had suggested we use the hour before dinner to *reflect and process*, but I needed a nap. I flopped on my thin mattress, pulled the gray fleece blanket over my head and curled up in a ball.

And, of course, for the first time in my life, I couldn't sleep.

Under the blanket, in my little cave, I opened my eyes. The INTRO logo stared me right in the face, embroidered in red and yellow stitching. I tried to remember what it stood for—In Nature something—and entertained myself by making up alternatives.

IDIOTIC NASTY TERRIBLE RIDICULOUS ORGANIZATION

ISLAND NONCONFORMISTS TORTURED REALLY OFTEN

I NEED TO REVOLT. OBVIOUSLY.

Yeah, good luck with that one, Alice. I pictured the two kayaks I'd seen pulled up on the rocky beach. Escape? Not a chance. Not over that distance, not with no land in sight, not with water this rough. It had taken over an hour to get here in a high-speed Zodiac. No way could I kayak to civilization. I was stuck here. I'd just have to do my time.

It was true, what I'd said to Caleb about my mother. I was here because of her paranoid imagination. She'd freaked out over the littlest thing, decided I was heading down the wrong path and was going to end up dropping out of school, selling my body, living on the streets—God knows what. *I love you way too much to stand by and watch you throw your life away,* she'd said.

You'd think she'd caught me shooting smack, not having a few beers at a party. I mean, I wanted to be a cop! A detective! I guess technically I was drinking underage, but everyone did that, and for the most part I was all about law enforcement. I certainly wasn't about to do anything that could get me a criminal record. *Holy drama, Batman,* I'd said.

Which pissed her off even more.

Hence INTRO.

Every time I thought about it, the rage bubbled up all over again. Sure, fine, she loved me—but she obviously didn't trust me. Either she thought I was lying to her about not needing help, or she thought I was an idiot who had a huge problem and didn't realize it. Either way, it was insulting. Either way, it pissed me off.

I could hear Mandy and Imogen talking in hushed voices, but I couldn't make out what they were saying. I sat up. "Where's Tara?"

"Making dinner," Imogen said. "She and Chad were first on the schedule."

"Oh yeah. Right." I was getting hungry. I hoped it was better than the afternoon snack. I had a bad feeling that Claire and Warren were vegetarian and we were all destined for a week of tofu and sprouts.

A bell rang loudly, calling us to the mess hall. Apparently I was about to find out.

* * *

Dinner was salad, brown rice and some sort of bean stew. No one talked much, except Chad, who seemed to be unable to shut up. I tuned him out and focused on the food. Vegetarian, but edible.

Tara was sitting beside me, but she disappeared into the washroom at the start of the meal, and Caleb slid into her empty chair. "Look, sorry if I offended you," he said. "About the karate thing. I mean, I get it. I hate when people make assumptions."

"It's okay." I guessed I should probably apologize for being a complete bitch. I took off my glasses and rubbed them with the corner of my shirt. "I've been in a foul mood since I stepped on that Zodiac, to be honest."

"I hear you." He nodded toward the washroom door. "Is she all right? Tara? Chad says she's a mess. Kept crying while they were doing the food prep."

"I dunno."

"I doubt whether spending time with Chad helped any," Caleb said. "Anyway, I guess I felt bad 'cause we said that thing about her being suicidal, you know?"

"You said it. Not me."

"Yeah. But, uh, if you get a chance to talk to her, it might not be a bad thing to check in, you know?"

"Nothing stopping you," I said.

"I thought maybe you'd have more luck. Being a girl, I mean."

"I doubt it." I put my glasses back on and looked up at him. Even sitting down, he was way taller than me, and I'd bet he weighed double what I did. "I'm not so good at that kind of thing."

"Well, maybe she'll talk to Rahim," Caleb said.

"Maybe. But if she isn't depressed now, she will be after a week of this bullshit." I folded my arms across my chest. "Why are you so concerned about her anyway?"

He just shrugged, and as if on cue, Tara emerged from the bathroom and walked back toward us, her eyes blood-shot and swollen and her shoulders hunched forward. Rahim stood and rang a bell to get everyone's attention.

"I hope you all enjoyed your first dinner on the island," he said. "We're going to be doing one of my favorite things this evening. Expressive art therapy!"

Caleb caught my eye and winked, and I looked away, my cheeks hot again. Not my type, I reminded myself. Too bad—a hookup would definitely be one way to make the week more bearable. Jason was good-looking in a bad-boy way—all flat planes and sharp angles and five-o'clock shadow—and the accent was dead sexy, but he seemed full of himself, which was a total turnoff. Nick was cute, but I had a feeling that any girl going after him was going to be disappointed.

And then there was Imogen. I closed my eyes and pictured her putting on her lipstick. Totally hot. I didn't think she was as messed up as she made herself sound— all her stories seemed to me like a way of keeping people at a distance. Yeah, she had some sharp edges, but underneath the prickles she seemed smart and funny. I wondered if she was straight, and if not, whether she assumed I was…

"Earth to Alice," Claire said. Was it my imagination, or was there a slight edge to her voice? Irritation or impatience hidden beneath the ever-present smile?

I shook off the thoughts and realized I was alone at the table—everyone was moving into the circle area and sitting down on the floor. "Sorry."

"It's okay. It's a lot to take in, arriving here." She lowered her voice. "It can be overwhelming, especially if you don't much like group activities."

"Uh, was it that obvious?" I was startled. I mean, I'd hated the group stuff, but I thought I'd been covering that up pretty well.

"Well, it's my job, working with people. And a lot of what I do is group work." She looked at me. "But I'm still nervous on the first day with each new group."

"Yeah?" Maybe that was what the phoniness was about. I still didn't trust her though.

"Yeah. Anyway, I have a confession to make. I'm not really that perceptive. I had inside information."

"Huh?"

"Your mother. On the registration form, she said you weren't much for groups, and she asked us to make sure you gave it a fair shot."

"Oh." *Thanks, Mom.*

"Warren told me he knows her," she said. "Diane, right? I must have met her—he said she was at our wedding, but you know how it is when you meet a lot of people all at once." One corner of her mouth quirked up. "It's a bit of a blur."

"Yeah. They worked together," I said. "Years ago. She's a police officer. Detective now, actually. Major Crimes Unit."

"Can't be easy. I mean, it's a pretty male-dominated profession, isn't it?"

"Yeah. I guess." A line from the INTRO website flashed into my mind. *Our highly trained staff will establish trust and rapport as a basis for growth and change.* Well, too bad for Claire. I wasn't interested in bonding. "Uh, I should join…" I nodded to the group.

"Yes. Try to relax, Alice. Rahim's an excellent therapist, and I think you'll enjoy the art exercises." She met my eyes. "If you let yourself."

I doubted it, but I headed over to the group and took my seat in the circle. We each chose a large sheet of Bristol board (red, blue, green, yellow or pink), and Rahim handed out glue sticks, markers, scissors and stacks of magazines.

"This is going to be a silent exercise," he told us. "I want you to be together, in this group, in community. Connected and supporting each other, but silently. Each of you on your own individual journey. So no talking, all right?"

Good. Silence suited me fine.

"I'm going to start you off with a visualization." He smiled. "Close your eyes and relax and just listen to my voice. You are lost at sea on a stormy night…"

"SERIOUSLY?" Imogen yelped. "Should they visualize me puking?"

I snorted a laugh. *Good one, Imogen.*

"Shhhh," Rahim said. "You are lost at sea, and you are cold and wet…but you see a glimmer of light. You know there is land not far off. If you row hard, you can make it. And there, onshore or maybe in a lighthouse, someone waits for you. There might be a hot meal or dry clothes. Perhaps there is a cozy fire crackling in the hearth. A steaming bath. A soft bed."

"With a hot chick in it?" Chad asked hopefully.

"Oh my god. Do you have to be such a pig?" I said.

Imogen gave a nod of agreement.

Rahim ignored us both. "Now I want you to look at the paper in front of you. You can draw, color, use the collage materials—whatever you like—to create an image of that shore or that lighthouse. That source of guidance and comfort and safety in your life. Make sure you include your-self somewhere in the image, in a boat on the water, in the lighthouse…it's up to you."

Chad flipped through a magazine, no doubt looking for someone to put in his imaginary bed. The rest of us just sat there. Imogen caught my eye, grinned and stuck out her pierced tongue.

Was she flirting with me? I was always so bad at telling.

* * *

In bed, after lights-out, I thought about what Caleb had said. I couldn't help wondering why he was so worried about Tara. I mean, sure, she seemed depressed, but it was unusual for a guy to be so…concerned. Maybe he knew someone who'd attempted suicide or something. Maybe he was scared she was going to do something to hurt herself. I sighed and sat up in bed. Good luck going to sleep now that I had that thought in my head.

Tara's bed and mine were on one wall of the cabin, Imogen's and Mandy's on the other. The cabin was inky dark, so I couldn't see the others, but someone was snoring softly.

"Tara," I whispered. "Are you awake?"

"Yeah," she whispered back. "You too? Obviously. Duh."

I sat up, swung my legs over the edge of my bed and, bringing my blanket with me for warmth, shuffled over to her bed. "Mind if I sit?"

"No. I don't think I'll ever get to sleep anyway." A pause. "I wouldn't mind company."

I perched on the end of her bed, not sure what to say. "Dinner was pretty good, wasn't it? I have to admit, I was worried it'd be mashed tofu with kale or something, but it wasn't bad at all."

"I like cooking." She sounded guilty, like she was admitting to some dark secret.

I was dying to ask her how she'd gotten herself sent here—hash brownies?—but I didn't want to sound nosy. "You were paired up with Chad, right?"

"Uh-huh." She didn't sound too enthusiastic.

"Seems like a dick."

"I guess." I could hear the shrug in her voice. "He's a pothead. I think he got arrested for dealing or something. I'm not into that stuff. Um. No offense, I mean, like if you're here for something like that. I just don't—"

"No, no. I mean, I know what you mean. And I'm— I guess we aren't supposed to talk about this?"

"Just not supposed to ask, I think."

"Whatever." I lowered my voice in case Imogen and Mandy were listening in. "I don't really care anyway. But I'm here for drinking too much at a party. Seriously, that's it."

"Uh-huh." She sounded like she didn't believe me.

"Honestly," I said. "My mom overreacted."

There was a long silence, and the darkness between us began to feel even darker. We started to speak at the same time.

"So you—" I began.

"And you're with Caleb, right?" she asked.

"*Caleb?* Me?" Then I realized what she meant. "Oh, for meal prep. Yeah."

"He's pretty cute," she said.

"Yeah, I guess." I dropped my voice to a whisper. "I'm waiting for Mandy to realize that Warren isn't available. She's going to be all over Caleb, don't you think?"

"I hope not. I mean, not because I'm interested."

I laughed. "Oh, of course not."

"No, seriously. I…I'm not looking for anything like that. But he seems really nice. He was nice to me anyway. He went out of his way to talk to me a couple of times. And…well, he seems really genuine and sincere, you know. And his art was really good."

"You think?" Caleb had looked pissed off about having to share his work, but the boy clearly had talent. Rahim had guided the discussion, and he'd asked us to share our own feelings and not comment on each other's art. He said it was about emotional expression, not artistic skill. Still, I had to admit I'd been impressed. Had to admit to myself, that is—I didn't see any reason to say so out loud. Not to Tara, and definitely not to Caleb.

I heard her yawn. "I'm gonna crash, okay?" she said. "Will you be able to sleep?"

"I've got a book," I said. "And a flashlight. I'm good."

I dragged myself and my blanket back over to my bed. The novel I'd brought along was beside my pillow, but my mind was all over the place, and there was no way

I could read. Besides, who needed dystopian fiction when the current reality was INTRO? This place was more than dystopian enough.

I curled up on my side and tried hard not to think about anything at all.

SUNDAY

FIVE
Caleb

I woke up in a foul mood. The wooden beds were tiny, and I'm six foot four. I hadn't slept in a bed this small since I was, like, ten. Mom gave me her queen-size mattress when Barry moved in and insisted on a king-size bed. I don't know why—he's only about five foot eight. I think that's one of the reasons I piss him off—I've got eight inches on him.

I've never really had to share a room with anyone either—no brothers or sister; my mom says I'm a limited-issue model—and I couldn't believe the amount of farting, belching and snoring those guys produced. We'd stayed up late after the art session the night before. Well, Chad stayed up and kept me and Jason and Nick awake. There was no set time for lights-out at INTRO. We were trusted to, as Rahim said, *monitor and regulate our own behavior.* I wondered if Rahim had ever actually spent any time with guys our age. *Monitor* and *regulate* were not words that sprang to mind.

Chad had smuggled some weed onto the island. *Butt-crack baggie*, he'd announced, pulling it out from under his mattress. *I figured they'd search our bags but probably not our butts.* He giggled. *Although that Rahim dude looks like he might enjoy that sort of thing. You guys in?*

That's disgusting, Nick said.

Nah, I'm knackered. Jason shook his head. *Feckin' thick, bringing that here.*

Weed gives me a wicked headache, so I said, *I pulled breakfast duty. I'm gonna turn in.*

Nick had turned away and started lining stuff up on the shelf beside his bed. Toothbrush, toothpaste, mouthwash, floss, comb, sunscreen, mosquito repellent, deodorant. His shoulders were hunched, and it looked as if his hands might be shaking a bit. I'd wondered what was freaking him out—the weed or the fact that Chad was a Grade A douche. Maybe both.

Jason climbed into bed and turned his back on all of us.

Soon Chad was cackling and playing air guitar and generally acting like a total jackass. The whole cabin stank of dope—Chad blew the smoke out the window, and the breeze blew it straight back in. I used the bathroom, stripped down to my T-shirt and boxers and climbed into my toddler bed. Nick disappeared into the bathroom for so long I got worried about him—a suicide on our first night would not be a good thing—but he eventually emerged and flopped into bed.

Then I lay awake, trying to find a way to get comfortable. The choices were limited. Eventually I dragged the mattress onto the floor and sprawled across it diagonally. My feet still hung off the end, but at least I wasn't bumping up against the headboard and footboard. A week of this and I'd probably a) become homicidal and b) need some serious physio.

We had been told to bring an alarm clock, since we weren't allowed to have phones, and mine (a Darth Vader digital I bought at a dollar store) woke me up at six. The other guys swore and threw stuff at me—a pillow, a pair of rank socks, a sleep mask—but by the time I was dressed, they had all gone back to sleep. The breakfast gong (which turned out to be an actual Chinese gong that hung outside the mess hall) would be rung at seven. One of the perks of being the chef, Warren had told us, was that you got to strike the gong. Otherwise, it was off-limits. Staff only. Infractions would be punished by unspecified physical torment. Warren grinned when he told us that, as if he knew that at least one person wouldn't be able to resist the temptation. I'd put my money on Chad being the one to make Warren's day.

If you didn't make your way to the dining room when the meal bell rang, you would be SOL until the next meal. Water and energy bars were available throughout the day, they told us, but everything else was on lockdown. If the gong sounded three times, it was time for a meeting. Five times meant there was an emergency, and we were to gather in the mess hall. Very military. I bet Warren would like it if we saluted him too. I could totally see the cop in him—eyes flicking from face to face, assessing, judging. I'd have to be careful around him. Wary. If he thought I was going to challenge him, he was wrong.

When I got to the kitchen, Alice was already there, cracking eggs into a huge bowl. She didn't look super happy to see me, but then, I probably looked the same. At least egg-white omelets and kale juice didn't seem to be on the menu.

"Scrambled eggs and bacon," she said. "That's what the menu says."

"Want me to start the bacon?" I asked. I actually like cooking. Mom hates it. Her idea of gourmet is Lean Cuisine instead of Hungry-Man. I started cooking long before it was safe for me to use the stove. Now Barry has taken over, and we eat like it's the 1950s. Meat and potatoes. No salads, no fish, no chicken. All red meat all the time. Almost makes me want to become a vegetarian.

The bacon was sitting on the counter, and I started laying it out on the grill. "Eleven people, right?" I said. "Three strips each? Four?"

"Whatever." She grabbed a whisk and started beating the bejesus out of the eggs. I wanted to tell her to stop—eggs get tough if you overbeat them—but I kept my mouth shut and watched the bacon cook.

"Where's the toaster?" I asked.

"Isn't one. I looked. I guess you have to use the grill."

We worked side by side in silence. I bit my tongue when she started to scramble the eggs over high heat. There were no paper towels, so I drained the bacon on a dishtowel, wiped down the grill and then started on the toast while Alice put out cutlery and dishes in the dining room. In a weird way, it was kind of okay—not talking, just doing what had to be done. I'm never big on chitchat, and I'm not an early-morning person. Seemed like Alice was the same. Or she really hated me. Either way, we worked together pretty well.

"Do you want to ring the gong?" I said when I had put the last of the bread on the grill. "Then we can get everything out onto the table while we wait for people to come."

She nodded and went outside. The gong sounded, deep and melodious in the morning stillness. Warren appeared in the dining room almost immediately, rubbing his meaty hands together and saying, "You can never go wrong with bacon!"

"Unless you're vegan," Alice said. I laughed, and Warren stopped shoveling eggs onto his plate and gave us both a beady stare. Maybe backtalk was banned on Therapy Island.

Within ten minutes, everyone else was there, slathering peanut butter on toast, guzzling juice, laughing when the plastic ketchup bottle made a fart noise (Chad again). When everyone was finished, Claire stood up and said, "How about a round of applause for our chefs, Alice and Caleb? Great job, guys." She started clapping, and everyone else joined in halfheartedly.

"You've got half an hour before we meet back here for our first group session. You might want to find somewhere to be alone—somewhere you can get in touch with your true self before we start the work we came here to do. Group work is hard. If you're going to get anything out of it, you're going to have to make yourselves vulnerable. Expose aspects of yourself that no one ever gets to see."

Chad leaned over and said something to Jason, who frowned and turned away.

Alice rolled her eyes at me, and I grinned back. No doubt Chad had just said something about how he'd like to expose himself to Claire.

Warren turned to Chad, forehead creased and eyebrows lowered in a deep frown. "It's in your best interests to take this seriously, son," and Chad muttered, "I'm not your son, dude."

"Right now, I'm all that's standing between you and a stint in juvie, bud," Warren replied. "So show some respect. Maybe if your own dad had given you more guidance as you were growing up, you wouldn't be here at all."

Chad stood up, took a couple of steps toward Warren and glowered down at him. "Leave my dad out of it. If he was here, he would kick your ass."

Maybe our pothead roomie wasn't so laid-back after all.

"Is that so?" Warren said. "Like this?" He calmly reached out one massive arm and immobilized Chad in a headlock.

Chad's eyes widened. Guess he hadn't seen that coming.

"Sit down and shut up," Warren said, depositing Chad back into his chair. He turned to the rest of us. "I don't like resorting to the use of physical force," he said, "but I will if I have to. Are we clear?"

No one said a word, since it sounded like a rhetorical question.

Claire clapped her hands, and I groaned. That was getting old really fast.

"Put your dirty dishes in the gray bins. Make cleanup as easy as possible for your chefs. You'll appreciate it when it's your turn."

She slid her own plate into one of the bins, and everyone followed suit. When Alice and I finished the cleanup, Rahim hit the gong three times, and people began filing back into the dining room for our first group session. The expressions on their faces ranged from sad (Tara) to sullen (Mandy) to apprehensive (Nick). I was happy to see that Warren was absent. Probably out devising some diabolical obstacle course or something.

SIX

Caleb

Once everyone was seated (in a circle, of course), Rahim led things off by saying, "Today is a good day to bury bad habits, attitudes and relationships so you can give birth to a new you." He smiled at us, his face open and so hopeful that I actually felt bad for the guy—I had a feeling we were about to disappoint him. Some people nodded, some looked at their shoes, some glowered at him. I picked at a blob of dried ketchup on my jeans.

"What if I like the old me?" Nick asked. He didn't sound pissed off or anything, just curious.

"Well, Nick," Rahim said, "I think you have to consider what it was about the old you that led you to this place."

"I'm here because my parents don't like the old me," Nick said. "They made up some total lie about finding drugs in my bedroom, which apparently INTRO believed, but the truth is, they think being here will toughen me up. Make a man of me, which is bullshit. I'm a man already. I'm just not the kind of man they want me to be."

"And what kind would that be, Nick?" Rahim asked.

"Straight," Nick replied.

There was a short silence, which Chad broke. "Ah, man," he said. "You mean I'm sharing a cabin with a fag?"

Practically everyone turned at the same time and glared at Chad, though I noticed Jason folded his arms across his chest and looked down at the ground like he wasn't too sure whose side he was on.

"Hey, it was a joke," Chad mumbled. "Shit. Lighten up."

We ignored him, which was already becoming a theme. There was silence for a moment, and then Tara said, "So basically your parents are homophobic and this is, like, one of those gay-conversion camps for you."

Nick nodded. "Sounds about right."

"And how does that make you feel?" Rahim asked.

Nick started to laugh. "You're about the sixteenth therapist who's asked me that. And I always say the same thing. It makes me feel shitty, but I can't change them any more than they can change me. So I just go with the flow. For now."

"Thank you for being so honest," Rahim said. "Before we go any further, Claire would like to talk about how we're going to structure these sessions."

Claire smiled at each of us in turn as she looked around the room. She must have learned the technique in therapy school—make each individual feel included, set the tone for the group—but it came off as fake.

"Now that Nick has led the way," she said, "I'm hoping we can continue in the spirit of openness and honesty as we share our stories. Today I'm going to ask you simply to listen to your fellow travelers"—someone snorted, and I figured it was Jason—"and refrain from comment. There will be plenty of time for that later." She held up a brown-paper grocery bag. "I'm going to pull three names out of this bag, and we'll provide a safe and nurturing space for those people to tell us their stories this morning. Then we'll have a break for lunch, followed by the final four. We have a zero-tolerance policy regarding any type of abuse—verbal, physical, emotional or sexual. We are here to support each other and promote change. And finally, I want to remind you that you have each signed a confidentiality agreement as part of your registration. It's important for everyone that you respect that policy."

"What goes on at INTRO stays at INTRO," Rahim added with a nervous smile. I wondered if Claire had told him to say that. He wasn't exactly a Vegas kinda guy.

"Bring on the strippers and coke!" Chad yelled. Everybody laughed, even Claire and Rahim.

Claire reached into the bag and pulled out three slips of paper. "Mandy, Imogen and Caleb. You're up. Anyone want to volunteer to go first?"

Silence.

Imogen fiddled with the piercing in her eyebrow, and Mandy crossed and uncrossed her long bare legs. We'd be here forever if I didn't get things rolling.

"My name's Caleb. I beat up my stepdad, and I got sent here because it was a first offense and I'm a juvenile. It's called diversion—keeps you out of the courts."

"Why did you beat up your stepdad?" Tara asked, earning a frown from Claire.

"Please refrain from commenting in this session, Tara," Claire said.

"I'm not commenting. I'm asking a question. There's a difference."

"Caleb, you don't have to answer," Claire said.

I shrugged. "I don't mind answering. I beat him up because I was tired of seeing him beat up my mom. She'd never have him charged. He'd always say he was sorry, and he'd promise to change. She always believed him. But one day he broke her jaw, and when we got back from the hospital, he told her to make his dinner and I lost it. He ended up in the hospital, and I ended up here. You can guess whose side my mom took." I stopped speaking. The memory of my mom dragging me off him and screaming, *Leave him alone, Caleb,* made me feel like puking.

"Thank you, Caleb," Rahim said. "Now, I want everyone to understand that you don't have to go into any more detail right now than you're comfortable with. This is a get-to-know-you session, not a therapy session. There will be lots of opportunity in our private sessions to explore things more deeply."

Claire nodded. "Who's next?"

Mandy recrossed her legs, stared down at her bright-pink toenails and sighed theatrically. "I'm here because

I'm an adrenaline junkie. I like doing crazy shit. Not stuff like mountain biking and skydiving—I'm so not a jock, and I don't want to, you know, hurt myself—but I'll do pretty much anything if you dare me to. Like stealing shit, or having sex in a public place. That's pretty cool."

I guarantee that every guy in the room—well, maybe not Nick—had a vivid image of Mandy up against the wall of a club bathroom, her long legs wrapped around some guy's waist, her back arched. I know I did, and Chad was almost drooling.

"Anyway," she continued, playing with a lock of hair that had come loose from her ponytail, "when I was little I took, like, a candy bar at the grocery store when no one was looking, and it was such a rush. It made me feel, I dunno, powerful or something. I had a secret—and candy. I graduated to lipstick and nail polish when I was about twelve, but when that started to get old, I ramped it up. Earrings, necklaces, rings—anything small enough to fit in my purse. Then I took something really valuable—a Rolex for my boyfriend—and got caught. The store owner let me off with a warning when I sobbed on his shoulder and told him I was a klepto—that stealing from him was a cry for help. He called my parents, and they sent me here."

"And was it?" Alice asked.

"Was it what?" Mandy said.

"A cry for help."

Mandy grinned. "Nope. I like the way it makes me feel. I just don't want to go to jail for it."

"Thank you for being so honest, Mandy," Claire said. "Imogen?"

Imogen sighed and said one word. "Drugs."

"Would you care to elaborate?" Claire asked.

"Lots of drugs."

Alice snickered, and Chad said, "Let me guess. A little weed, maybe some E on the weekends?"

Imogen couldn't resist the urge to put Chad in his place. "Started smoking weed when I was eleven. My stepbrother gave it to me. He's getting his MBA now. Totally boring dude. Back then he got high all the time, mostly to piss off our dad. Weed was all he did though. Unlike me. You name it, I've done it. Crack, E, blow, acid, mushrooms, even meth, but I don't do that shit anymore. Messed me up pretty bad for a while, although I did lose a lot of weight." She laughed. "Total upside, am I right?"

No one said anything, although we were probably all wondering how she got off meth—she wasn't skinny, and she actually looked pretty healthy. Her skin was pale but unmarked by even a single zit. Her eyes, ringed with black makeup, were clear, and her teeth were white and even. Maybe those stories she told Alice were bullshit. Maybe she was still lying. But then, why was she here?

"I got busted with a quarter gram and sent to rehab. A really expensive rehab in the desert in California. It was pretty cool. More like a spa, really. My mom's a total bitch, but she wasn't about to send me to some crappy local rehab. What if her friends found out? With me in California, she could tell them anything she wanted. I think she usually said I was at an ashram or something, getting my chakras aligned and doing yoga 24-7. Which is hilarious. Do I look like I do yoga?" No one said anything. "Anyway," she continued, "I stopped doing meth, which was the whole point of rehab. Gold star for Imogen. As soon as I got out, I started smoking heroin. Chasing the dragon. I didn't do needles, ever, just smoked it." She thrust out her arms and pulled up the sleeves of her black sweater. Her arms were smooth and plump and unmarked. "No track marks, see?"

Right, I thought. No proof she was telling the truth either.

"Everything was cool until my best friend—well, I thought she was my best friend—told my mom what I was doing. And my mom called my dad, even though she hates him, and they decided to send me here. Like I was a junkie or something. Which I'm totally not. I never get *hooked* on anything. I just like getting high."

She leaned back in her chair and folded her arms across her chest.

"Thank you, Imogen," Claire said. "And thank you, Caleb, Nick and Mandy for sharing your stories. We're going to take a break now, get out into nature and reconvene after lunch. Take some time to process what you've heard. Let kindness and compassion guide your thoughts. Rahim and I will be in the staff cabin if anyone needs to debrief. Otherwise, enjoy the sunshine and listen for the lunch bell."

She pulled the hair band off her ponytail and shook her head so that her brown hair tumbled around her shoulders. "I'm going to get some fresh air myself," she said, flashing her white teeth at us in a wide smile.

Maybe I was being overly harsh, but something about Claire rubbed me the wrong way. She sounded like she was reading from a script. Rahim was obviously inexperienced and insecure, which didn't inspire confidence, but he did at least seem sincere.

I headed back to the cabin to take a leak and grab my notebook, which was about the size of one of those big iPhones. Small enough to hide, which was a habit I'd gotten into after Barry ripped up most of my sketches during one of his rages.

I walked down to the beach where the kayaks were stored, took out my notebook and a fine-tip black pen, and started drawing. Mandy's legs, Alice's almost-albino eyebrows, Imogen's smooth arms. I worked fast, in case someone else appeared on the beach. Drawing was something I needed to do—an outlet, I guess. A way of making sense of the world.

And it was also my secret. Warren, Claire and Rahim might spend the week prying and making us talk about our personal business, but some things were private. No one here knew the big dumb jock could capture someone with a few rapid pen strokes. I intended to keep it that way.

SEVEN

Alice

The morning was the longest one of my life. Group-session hell. I felt like a snail surrounded by birds, all pecking at me and trying to pry me out of my shell with their hooked beaks.

If you don't talk constantly—especially if you don't want to share your innermost thoughts and feelings with every random person—people figure you just need encouragement. That of course you must—*deep down*—be dying to spill. But I've never been like that. I don't *want* to be like that. I'm not shy. Just private.

We took a short break before lunch, and I went for a walk in the woods—by myself, thank God. Both Imogen and Mandy hinted that they wouldn't mind going with me, but I managed to shake them off. Mandy was a total ditz, and Imogen…well, I didn't quite know what to make of Imogen. There was a certain energy between us that made me feel flustered and self-conscious.

Besides, I really needed the time alone.

I had told Caleb I wasn't much of a nature girl, and it was true, but it wasn't like I hated being outdoors. My mom and I camped most summers, and I loved the lakes in the interior, and the Rocky Mountains, and the wild west-coast beaches with crashing waves. But this island? There was nothing beautiful about it. It was sparse and scrubby, the trees a bit bare and stunted-looking until you got a little ways into the woods—and then it was dark and clammy and full of mosquitoes. The place felt creepy. Too silent, so every little noise made me jump. We were so cut off from everything here.

I couldn't believe how much I missed my phone.

When the gong sounded, I was tempted to ignore it and skip lunch, but I decided not to take the risk. Not because I'm a rule follower, like Caleb said, but because I couldn't face the extra analysis that would probably result. Besides, much as I had wanted to be alone, I was too spooked to enjoy it.

So I headed in for lunch, ate my salad and veggie wrap, then trooped back into the circle of hell known as group therapy.

Half a day down. Six and a half to go.

"Alice," Claire said, "would you like to go next?"

I pulled my feet up in front of me on the hard wooden chair. My butt bones already hurt from sitting in it. Claire's teeth glinted at me, Crest-strip white. She was smiling like she thought we had a bond now. She was wrong.

"Not particularly," I said, and I saw her eyes narrow slightly although her smile never wavered.

"I will," Jason said.

I glanced across the circle at him, and he gave me a lazy grin. He was cute, but he knew it. Full of himself, I thought again, deliberately meeting his eyes and not smiling or winking back. I hoped he could tell I wasn't impressed.

Jason leaned forward in his chair. "Might as well get it over with, right?"

Rahim beamed at him. "Always a good idea to step forward. To confront your fears head on, bravely, knowing that you have the strength to—"

"Yeah yeah." Jason stretched his legs out in front of him. He was one of those guys who liked to take up a lot of space, as if he was trying to make up for being short. "Sure, it's no big thing. I broke into some places. Stole some stuff. Electronics mostly." He cleared his throat. "Got caught. End of story."

"Thank you, Jason," Rahim said. "But of course, it's not the end of the story, is it? Because here you are. And you have your whole life ahead of you. And you didn't just decide to start breaking into houses on a whim. Everything we do, everything we are, is, well, it's…" He trailed off as if he'd lost his train of thought.

Claire bailed him out. "And there'll be time this week to explore all of that in more depth."

"Right, right." Rahim nodded so fast you could have shaken a James Bond martini in his skull. "I mean, we do things because…"

"Because reasons," Caleb said solemnly.

"Because money," Jason said.

"You sell the stuff?" Mandy asked.

"My older brother does. It's a family business. Steal from the rich, give to the poor. The poor, in this case, being my family."

Claire stepped in swiftly. "Thank you, Jason. Thank you for sharing your story. Who's next? Alice? Chad? Tara?"

She sure liked to be in charge. If you asked me, that warm-and-perky manner covered up some serious control issues.

Tara and I exchanged glances. I knew she didn't want to share any more than I did.

"Uh, I'll go, I guess." Chad sat up a bit and brushed his stringy hair off his face. It looked like he hadn't washed it in a year, and I didn't even want to imagine how gross it must feel. Or smell. Ugh. "Court condition," he said. "I was selling some weed, that's all. Primo BC bud too—wicked-quality stuff. Arctic Sun. It should be legal already—"

"But it isn't," Claire cut in.

"Yeah, no shit. That's what the judge said too. So…" He shrugged. "It was INTRO or juvie. Pretty much a no-brainer."

"Just as well," Imogen said, trying to catch my eye.

I wanted to laugh, but I was too distracted by the thought that either Tara or I had to go next. "I'll go," I blurted.

"Thank you, Alice," Rahim said. "We are here to share this journey with you. Thank you for trusting us."

Did I say I trusted them? I was pretty sure I hadn't said anything of the sort. "I'm here because I drank too much at a party. Too much, in this case, meaning four beers."

"Four beers?" Chad laughed. "Dude, you were just getting started!"

I made a face. "We were playing this drinking game, Bullshit. Get caught bullshitting, you drink."

"I take it you're a bad liar?" Imogen said.

I nodded. "Yeah. Four beers in less than an hour. Then I threw up and passed out and someone called my mom. And I ended up in the emergency room with alcohol poisoning."

"After four beers?" Chad was, apparently, stuck on this.

Caleb gave him a shove. "She's, like, eighty pounds, dipshit."

I scowled at him, remembering his crack about me being anorexic. I ate plenty. It wasn't my fault I was small.

"No commenting, please," Claire reminded us. "Alice, was it a single incident? Or was there a pattern of behavior that led your mother to feel concerned?"

Obviously she had read my intake forms. So *obviously* she knew the answer to this. "You mean, have I got drunk at parties more than once? Of course I have." I looked around the circle. "Hands up if you've never gotten drunk at a party."

Tara's hand went up slowly, halfway.

"See?" I said. "Practically everyone does. It doesn't mean it's an issue. My mom, she's a cop. She sees all the worst-case scenarios. And it's always been just the two of us, you know? She's overprotective."

"Well, Alice, it sounds like you don't see your drinking as a problem," Rahim said. "And yet you ended up in a situation that could easily have been fatal."

Yikes. He'd nailed it. Rahim, one; Alice, zero. I swallowed hard. "Yeah. Yeah, I know."

"How does that make you feel?" he asked.

Stupid. Mortified. Humiliated. Ashamed. "Like I should probably avoid drinking games," I said lightly. It wasn't a lie. Drinking games are a bad idea when you have a serious competitive streak and most of your friends are guys twice your size. I hated letting guys beat me at anything. But I'd heard the stories of teens dying after games of Beer Pong or whatever, and I knew I'd dodged a bullet. I wasn't an idiot—I didn't need INTRO to remind me not to do it again.

Rahim sighed. He was probably disappointed with my utter shallowness. "Tara," he said. "You're the last to share. Would you like to tell the group why you are here?"

EIGHT
Alice

I looked at Tara, feeling bad for her before she even opened her mouth. Everything about her—the way her shoulders were hunched forward, the blotchy flush on her cheeks, the twisting fingers in her lap—screamed discomfort.

"Um. Yeah." She didn't say anything for a long moment, and the silence in the room grew heavy. I found myself thinking about Caleb, how he'd asked me to talk to her, and I glanced across at him. He was watching Tara, and there was something odd about his expression. Sort of analytical, like he was memorizing her features or something. Then, as if he sensed me looking at him, he turned toward me and our eyes met, and the thoughtful look was gone. Maybe I'd imagined it.

"I guess because I've been depressed," Tara said. "For a while. For a long time, really. But then...then last year someone really close to me died. And I guess I kind of fell apart."

My heart gave a funny little thud. *Please don't let it be her mother who died.* That was my worst nightmare. As furious as I was with her right now, I couldn't stand the thought of anything happening to my mother. Whenever there was a news story about a police officer getting killed, everything inside me went completely haywire with fear. If Tara's mom had died, I didn't want to hear about it.

Tara raked her fingers through her long dark hair. She had this habit of pulling it forward across her cheek, and I wondered if it was because she was self-conscious about her birthmark. It didn't look bad or anything, but she'd probably been teased about it when she was younger. Kids are such jerks.

"I was already depressed," she said. "As long as I can remember, really. But when I was in eighth grade I met someone. Right after my grandfather died and Gran and I had moved to Vancouver." Tara had been pretty quiet since we got to the island, but now it was like a switch had been hit, or a door opened. The words started pouring out like she couldn't say it all fast enough. "I know this sounds crazy, because we were so young, but he was my soul mate. We understood each other. We were best friends for a couple of years, but I always knew we'd end up together. And we did. We basically grew from best friends to being a couple, and I figured eventually we'd get married. We'd be together forever."

She looked up, looked around the circle, and there was something defiant in her gaze. "I don't care if some of you don't believe me. It's the truth. We were like…like two halves of an equation. We just went together."

"I believe you," Imogen said. Her voice was soft, the usual sharp edge totally absent.

Tara gave her a sad smile, looking grateful for the support. "He'd been depressed too," she said. "His family had some problems. Nothing huge—I mean, it was huge for him, but it was ordinary stuff. His parents had split up. He was getting counseling, and he seemed okay. He seemed like he was getting better. And then…something changed."

"Let it out," Rahim said, his voice a little hoarse. "Let it out."

I looked at Rahim and was startled to see that he actually had tears in his eyes.

"I didn't know what was wrong," Tara said. "But he started acting strange. Lying to me. About stupid things. Where he was. Who he was talking to. And I"—her voice caught, and she gulped loudly before going on—"I accused him of cheating on me." She looked around the circle, and I thought her gaze landed longest on Caleb. "I wish I hadn't. I thought…I thought he'd deny it. I wanted him to deny it—"

"But he didn't," Mandy said. "Shocker."

"No commenting," Claire put in.

"Tara, you confronted him?" Imogen asked. "And he admitted that he'd been cheating?"

She nodded. "He admitted it." A tear streaked down her cheek, and she wiped it away quickly. "But he wouldn't tell me who with. And it didn't even make any sense. I mean, we had a small group of friends, but we were together all the time, and no one acted weird or anything." She shrugged. "He said it was no one I knew. But I knew everyone he knew. I mean, we'd been like this"—she held up crossed fingers— "since we were thirteen."

"So hurtful," Rahim said. "It sounds as though you felt a profound sense of loss and betrayal. It takes time to heal from such deep wounds."

Tara stared at him. "No. No, that's not it at all. I FREAKED OUT. I lost it. I screamed at him and blamed him for the fact that I was such a mess." She pushed up the long sleeve of her hoodie. Her forearm was tiger-striped with horizontal scars—thin silver lines and recent ones that were red and angry-looking. "I told him it was his fault I'd started cutting again. I said he was as bad as his dad— throwing away something good for a stupid fling."

"Well, Tara, you had a right to be angry," Claire said. "You had a right to express your feelings."

Tara glared back at her. "Noah *killed* himself," she said. "He threw himself in front of a train, okay? He killed himself because of what I said. Did I have a right to do *that* to him?"

Claire looked stunned. She opened her mouth, but nothing came out. I guessed that little tidbit must've got left off Tara's registration form.

Rahim leaned forward. "Tara, losing someone to suicide is always devastating, but it is never the fault of the survivor. Your boyfriend—Noah—he made a choice. And you can't hold yourself responsible for that choice."

"That's what everyone tells me," Tara said. "It doesn't help. I'm always going to blame myself."

There was a really long silence. Then Mandy broke it. "Maybe it was *her* fault."

Jason, who was sitting beside her, gave her a shove. "Bloody hell, Mandy!"

Mandy shoved him back, only her shove looked more like an excuse to check out Jason's biceps. "Not her Tara. *Her*. The chick he was having the fling with. Maybe she did something."

"I don't think speculation is really going to be helpful," Claire said briskly. "Let's focus on how Tara is feeling and what we can do to support her."

Chad ignored Claire and focused on Mandy. "Like what? She dumped him, so he offed himself?"

Mandy threw up her hands impatiently. "Dumped him, gave him an STD, threatened to tell Tara. Whatever. I'm just saying, you don't *know*, right? There was this big secret thing in his life that you know shit-all about, so how can you be so sure about why he died?"

"That's enough," Claire said.

Tara ignored her. Her mouth was hanging slightly open, her eyes fixed on Mandy. "You're right. I mean, you're right that I don't know the whole story. Noah wouldn't tell me anything about her…" She pressed two fingers against her lower lip. "He kept a journal, you know? Hardly any guys do that, but he'd kept one since eighth grade. After he died, his mom and I looked, but we couldn't find it."

"Moving *on*," Claire said firmly. "Tara, thanks for sharing your story. How can we support you?"

Tara lifted her chin. "I think Mandy's right. I need to know the whole story. Who Noah was messing around with, what she did to him."

Claire shook her head. "Let's focus on your feelings, your—"

"They would've emailed each other," Nick said suddenly. "Or texted. Snapchat, Messenger, whatever. Have you checked his email?"

Tara shook her head slowly. "No. I didn't. I can't believe I didn't even think of that. I think I even know most of his passwords, unless he changed them—"

"Well, I'm afraid that will have to wait," Claire broke in. "You're a long way from home right now. No Wi-Fi, no cell reception. So perhaps, in the meantime, we could stop playing detective and focus on healing."

Playing detective? Seriously? People were trying to help Tara, and Claire's response was to mock them. Nice.

"Which brings me to our next activity," Claire said. "We're going to do a simple ritual together. A ceremony of sorts." She smiled, but it looked forced. I wondered if other people being helpful actually bugged her. Was she such a control freak that she wanted to be the only one who could help? And if so, why run groups? I mean, wasn't helping each other the point of a group?

She looked at Rahim, who jumped up and began to walk around the circle, handing each person a sheet of paper.

Claire crossed her legs and leaned back in her chair. "The key to letting go of the past is to embrace and accept it," she said.

"Hey, dude. This one's blank," Chad said, trying to hand his paper back.

"They all are, Chad. I want you each to write down one thing—one thought, one feeling—that keeps you stuck in the past." Claire paused. "Pens, Rahim?"

Rahim passed a jar of pens around the circle. I took one and wrote GROUP THERAPY SUCKS on my paper.

"And now I'll walk you through the steps to fold these pages into paper boats," Claire said. "First, like this…"

And a few minutes later we all had little paper boats and were trooping down to the beach to release them to the sea.

* * *

The ritual was totally corny. Still, I was happy to be outdoors and moving my body instead of trapped in circle time. The sky was gray and overcast and the air felt heavy, like it might rain any second. I shivered, chilled. My thin hoodie was basically useless.

We were supposed to be walking single file, in *contemplative silence*, but I ran a few steps and caught up to Nick.

"Hey." He nodded at me.

"Hey. I just…Claire's going to tell me to shut up any sec, but I wanted to say that it totally sucks, why you're here. I mean, that your parents are asshats about you being gay."

"Yeah. To be honest, I spend most of my time at my aunt's place."

"And she's cool?"

"Very. And she has a very cool little kid, Kelsey, who thinks I'm the greatest." He gave me a lopsided grin. "At least the guys didn't all flip out about sharing a cabin with me, right?"

"Jesus, yeah, no kidding." I hadn't even thought of that. "Though…you think if I told the other girls I was bi, they'd freak out? Like, enough that INTRO would send me home?"

His eyes widened in surprise. "You could try it." Then he turned and looked at me, head tilted, a half smile on his face. "Are you actually bi?"

"Actually bi. Or, you know, pan." I held up a fist, and he bumped it with his. "Queer solidarity, etcetera, etcetera. But my mom's cool with it, so it's no big thing."

Rahim tapped me on the shoulder and held his finger to his lips. "Shhhh."

I nodded and shut up. We were at the beach anyway.

Boat-launch time.

NINE
Caleb

The boat-launching thing was lame. My boat said *I enjoyed beating Barry up*. It wasn't something I was proud of, but it was true. When my fist smashed into his nose and blood gushed down his idiotic Def Leppard T-shirt, I felt like I could hit him forever. Maybe I would have if my mom hadn't started screaming and pulling me off him. Maybe I would have killed him. I was angry enough. So that was my dirty little secret—I am capable of extreme violence. I can't avoid that now, although I'd never hit anybody before except on the football field.

But what good does it do to send a paper boat out to sea? Especially when your boat only makes it about two feet before it sinks, taking your nasty secret with it. I know, I know. So symbolic.

After my boat sank, I watched Alice and Nick launch theirs. They were all fist-bumpy and buddy-buddy, putting their boats on the water at the same time, watching as a breeze propelled them past my poor sunken blob. Alice's probably said *I love getting wasted*. Nick's? That was tough. Maybe *There's nothing wrong with me. I'm here because people are morons.* Mandy was dancing around at the water's edge, shrieking when the water touched her toes. Her sandals were ridiculous: high-heeled and sparkly. I couldn't wait to see what she would wear when we started clearing brush with Warren. I'd put money on Daisy Dukes, a crop top and platform sneakers. I bet her boat said something like *I should have screwed that hot guy at Lucky Bar last week.* Chad's boat would be blank. Jason's might say *The rich deserve everything they get*, and Imogen would scribble *This place sucks* and leave it at that.

I couldn't think of anything for Tara though. Her story was so sad. I couldn't even imagine how it felt to lose someone that way, to blame yourself. It was weird that Claire and Rahim had let people discuss what had happened to Tara. It was almost like they had changed the rules for her. I watched her take off her shoes, roll up her jeans and wade into the water. I could see her lips move as she gently lowered her boat onto the water. She stood with her back to everyone for quite a while. When she finally turned around, it was clear she'd been crying. Her feet were almost blue when she got back to the beach and sat down on a log to put on her shoes.

"Pretty cold," I said. It was starting to rain too—fat, heavy drops splatting on the stony beach and dimpling the surface of the water.

She nodded. "I'm used to it."

She didn't volunteer anything else, so I asked, "Did you grow up on the water?"

She nodded again. "Salt Spring Island. With my grandparents. My grandpa swam in the ocean every single day. He taught me how to swim when I was really little. As soon as I could keep up, I went with him. Every day, no matter what. He said it would make me tough. He died a few years ago when we were out swimming. He had a stroke. I almost drowned trying to get him to shore." Tara took a deep, shaky breath before she continued. "After the funeral my grandma sold the house on Salt Spring, and we moved into a condo in Vancouver." She bent over and fiddled with the laces on her runners. I think she was trying to hide her tears. "I hate the water now. I won't go in past my knees."

"I'm sorry," I said. "He sounds like a cool guy."

"Yeah, he was." She unrolled her jeans and stood up. "I miss him. But he was wrong. All that swimming didn't make me tough. I think I'm the opposite of tough, really. I'm always afraid."

There was something so bleak about her expression that I felt a little scared myself. "Afraid?" I said.

She wrapped her arms around herself. "Oh, you know. Just life." She gave me a half smile before heading off. I followed her, not talking but feeling unsettled.

Claire and Rahim were stirring up all this stuff, and I didn't trust that they really knew what to do with it. I hoped INTRO wasn't going to make things worse for Tara.

* * *

After a dinner of vegetarian chili (heavy on the beans), you can imagine how awesome it was to be in a small cabin with three other guys. Not that I wasn't contributing, but when Chad started talking about the girls—how he'd like to bang Mandy, and how Imogen was probably a dyke—I said, "You guys play poker?" and he shut up. Turned out Nick and Jason were into it, but Chad had never played. Probably wouldn't be able to keep the suits straight anyway.

I got my cards and chips out of my bag. I'd figured I'd probably find someone to play with at INTRO, since all our devices had to be left at home. What else were we going to do? Play Pin the Tail on the Psycho? I wouldn't put it past Rahim to come up with some sort of therapeutic twist on Charades though. I shuddered as I shuffled the cards.

"Texas Hold'em?" I asked. "What are you guys in for?"

"A buck," Nick said.

"Hardly worth playing," I said. "How about five? Make it more interesting." I got out my wallet and plunked a five on the table.

"You some kind of hustler?" Jason said, pulling a five out of his pocket.

I shook my finger at him, laughing. "Would I tell you if I was?"

"Good point," Nick said, adding his five to the pile.

Chad got up and said, "This blows. I'm gonna go see whether Mandy wants to come out and play."

"Seriously?" I said. "It's pissing rain out there."

Chad leered and grabbed his crotch.

"Stupid ass," Jason said when Chad was gone. "Hope Warren busts him."

I hadn't been sure what to make of Jason, but my feelings toward him warmed a little. When it came to Chad, at least, we were on the same page. "Unless Warren has the same idea," I said. "Sneaking out after Claire starts to snore…"

"Gross," Nick said. "You really think Mandy would be into it?"

I shrugged. "Maybe. She gets off on that shit, right?"

"I wonder." Nick looked at his hand and smiled. "Not that I know much about girls."

We played for a couple of hours. Jason won the pot. Turned out he was more of a hustler than I was, but Nick was really hard to read too. When we decided to turn in, Chad still wasn't back. It was getting pretty dark outside, and the rain was getting harder too—it sounded like thunder on the cabin roof. I sure wouldn't want to be out there in it.

"Maybe he got lucky," Nick said.

Jason snorted. "Or he fell in the ocean and forgot how to swim."

The guy was growing on me.

MONDAY

TEN

Caleb

When I woke up the next morning, it was early—just past six o'clock. I slipped out of bed and went down to the beach with my sketchbook. The water was calm after the rain overnight, and the sky was a clear pale gray, like it had been washed clean. I sketched for a while, letting my mind clear. I love early morning—how quiet it is. I lost track of time, but eventually my stomach started to growl with hunger. I glanced at my watch. Almost eight, but the breakfast gong hadn't sounded. Or I'd sketched right through it.

Then I remembered that Chad and Tara were supposed to be cooking breakfast. Something told me we'd be eating cold cereal if I didn't get Chad moving. I made my way back to the cabin, and there he was, sound asleep on top of his blankets, fully clothed and still damp-looking, with his pillow over his head. He groaned when I prodded him with my foot and reminded him that he was on breakfast duty.

"The hell with breakfast," he said. "I hate breakfast. Tara can handle it."

"Your funeral," I said as I left.

I was almost at the dining hall when Imogen came flying out the door. She looked as if she had just leaped out of bed—hair wild, makeup smudged, plaid pajama pants and a wrinkled blue T-shirt. Bare feet.

She stopped running when she saw me. "Have you seen Tara?" Her breath came in gasps; she was seriously out of shape if running a few steps made her hyperventilate. Mind you, physical fitness probably wasn't high on her to-do list.

"Tara? No. Why?" I realized why Imogen looked so different: the usual bright-red lipstick was missing.

"She's gone. She was in the cabin last night with us, and this morning she was gone."

"Maybe she got up early to explore. That's what I did."

Imogen shook her head. "No. She was stoked about being on breakfast duty—buckwheat pancakes with blueberry sauce—so there's no way she would have been late for that. And Chad isn't in the kitchen either."

"Yeah, about that," I said. "Chad's in bed. Dead to the world."

"Why am I not surprised? Claire's in our cabin, trying to calm Mandy down—she's acting like it's all about her. How she wasn't nice enough to Tara, how if she'd just reached out…" Imogen rolled her eyes. "Like that would have helped. Alice was the last one to talk to Tara, and she's feeling really bad because she heard a noise in the night and didn't get up to investigate. Rahim and Warren are searching the island right now. I guess they want to make sure Tara's not sitting on a log somewhere before they call for help. Not good PR for INTRO if they lose a kid on the third day." She paused to catch her breath. "Claire sent me to get you guys to help check all the buildings. Can you get the others to help? Alice and I will stay here in case Tara turns up."

I nodded and headed back toward the guys' cabin. I remembered Tara telling me that she was always afraid. I wished I'd asked her, *Afraid of what?* Herself? Somebody else? Was she really suicidal? Or was she just hunkered down somewhere, avoiding group therapy? If so, I might join her.

"Tara's missing. We need to help look for her," I said when I opened the door to the guys' cabin.

Jason sat up and rubbed his face. "Missing? Like…what? Sorry, man. I'm not awake."

"She wasn't in the cabin this morning when the other girls woke up," I said. "And no one has seen her since last night. Warren and Rahim are out running around the woods. Claire's dealing with Mandy, who's freaking out. We need to search the buildings."

Nick grunted and staggered to the bathroom while Jason pulled on his jeans. Chad remained where he was, face down, pillow over his head. I yanked the pillow off and said, "Get up."

He rolled over and smiled up at me. A slow, lazy, try-and-make-me grin. "Maybe she followed her boyfriend to wherever losers go after they off themselves." He yawned and stretched his arms over his head. "All that shit about it not being her fault. Chick like that was lucky to get laid even once. Dude probably killed himself because she was so damn ugly."

I grabbed his T-shirt and hauled him to his feet. Rage surged through me. One punch. That's all it would take. Maybe two. I wanted to see fear in his eyes. I wanted him to hurt. A little blood would be a bonus.

Chad smirked. "Gotta work on those anger-management issues, man. I'm sure Rahim would be happy to give you some private sessions."

"Let's go, Caleb," said a voice at my side. Nick laid his hand on my arm.

"Saved by the fag. How ironic," Chad muttered and fell back onto his bed.

"Let's go," Nick said again. "Jason, you coming, man?"

Jason came out of the bathroom. "You're an asshole, you know," he said to Chad before he strode out the door.

Chad laughed and flipped Jason off.

"There are only two outbuildings," I said when we were outside. "Jason, can you check the one near the girls' cabin? Nick and I will look in the one behind the staff cabin. Meet you back at the mess hall."

Jason nodded and jogged away. Nick and I made our way to a small shed that turned out to contain axes, machetes, shovels, pickaxes, handsaws, safety goggles, flashlights—everything we would need for clearing brush, I guessed—but no Tara.

Jason returned and reported that the other shed was full of stuff like kayak paddles, life jackets, rope, a ladder, a generator and some tools—hammer, pliers, screwdrivers. Nothing strange. No Tara. When he mentioned rope, though, I had a sudden vision of Tara swinging from a tree in the dense woods, her feet still blue. How many ways were there to kill yourself on this island? Drowning was probably out—she was terrified of water, she'd said. Had there been any poison in the shed? I didn't think so, but she might have taken something from here, found a spot deep in the woods. Ended the pain.

Or she could have smuggled something from home. Pills or a razor…there were so many ways to die.

I swallowed hard. "We should do a perimeter search. Check out the shoreline. Maybe she got stranded by the tide or something." Even though Rahim and Warren were already searching, we couldn't just stand here and wait.

Nick nodded. "Okay. How about Jason and I go west from the dock and you go east?"

I took off at a run, almost twisting an ankle on the slippery rocks, calling Tara's name. I could hear Jason and Nick doing the same. On cop shows, searchers move methodically, examining the terrain and looking for microscopic clues. Maybe I should have done that, but all I could think of was covering as much ground as possible, looking behind every pile of driftwood, hoping to see Tara huddled down smoking a cigarette, maybe, or reading a book of poetry— she seemed like the poetry type. Not missing, just AWOL.

But she wasn't anywhere I looked. I had to turn back once I came to a rocky outcropping topped with dense brush. Short of swimming around it, there was no way to get to the other side.

The gong rang as I made my way back along the beach. One. Two. Three. Four. Five. Emergency meeting in the dining hall. That couldn't be good. Or could it? Maybe Tara had turned up, wondering what we were freaking out about. Or maybe this whole thing had been some bizarre test that the counselors had come up with. An experiment to see how we'd cope under stress. Maybe Tara had never really been missing at all. I started to run again, arriving back at camp just as Nick and Jason appeared from the other direction, shaking their heads.

It was pretty clear, once we got to the dining hall, that there wasn't any good news. Tara was nowhere to be found. Not on the west side of the island, not on the east, not in the woods, not anywhere. And, worst of all, one of the kayaks was missing. How had I not noticed that?

We stood around, basically saying the same things over and over. Everyone looked worried. Mandy's eyes were red from crying, Rahim was biting his cuticles, and Claire was so pale she looked ill. If this was something the counselors had cooked up, they were awfully good actors.

Even tough-guy Warren was shifting from foot to foot, gnawing on his bottom lip as he tried to sound calm. "She can't have gone far," he said. "We'll find her, I'm sure. Maybe she just went for a paddle and got farther away than she meant to."

"She would never do that," I said.

"Never do what?" Claire asked.

"Go out on the water. She was terrified of drowning."

"That's true," Alice said. "She told me the same thing."

"Well, a kayak is gone, so that's where we're going to start," Warren said.

"Shouldn't you call the coast guard or something?" Jason asked.

"We think that's premature," Claire said.

"Premature!" Alice yelped. "She's MISSING! As in GONE! Don't you even care that she might have killed herself? You people are unbelievable! Especially you, Warren. You used to be a cop. You know better than this. This place should be shut down!"

Claire smacked both hands down on the table in front of her. "Stop it! Alice, sit down. We have the situation under control. Caleb, please go and make something for us to eat. Rahim, you can help him. Cereal, toast—it doesn't matter. We're all hungry and tired and overwrought. Let's not make this worse than it already is. Girls, set the tables. And someone go and get Chad."

"Unless he's missing too," Imogen said.

"We should be so lucky," I said.

"Don't be so mean, guys," Mandy said. "It's not funny. What if they're both dead? What if there's, like, a serial killer on the island?"

"Don't be ridiculous, Mandy," Claire said. "That kind of hysteria helps no one. I'm sure Tara is fine."

Her words fell into a sudden awkward silence. I looked around at everyone standing there in the dimness of the mess hall. For a second I imagined sketching this scene— all those open mouths, those wide eyes, those pale, worried faces. The fear.

I didn't think anyone believed that Tara was fine.

"We should at least be out searching," Alice said again. "While we wait for the coast guard or the cops or whatever. Who you should already have called."

She might have been annoying, but when it came to speaking truth to power, the girl was fearless. I couldn't help respecting that.

"Warren and I will continue the search while you eat," Claire said. "We have procedures in place for emergencies like this, I assure you. I need you all to stay calm and let us do our jobs."

"Procedures. As if," Alice said.

"Not helpful, Alice," Warren snapped. "Claire and I will search. Rahim will stay here. Are we clear?"

"But if you don't find her—"Alice persisted.

"That's enough, Alice," Warren said. "Claire, let's head out. You good, Rahim?"

Rahim and I made a pile of toast and set it out on the tables with butter, peanut butter, jam and bananas. When Chad slouched into the room and sat at one of the tables, no one spoke to him. No one offered him a piece of toast.

He yawned loudly. "I could murder some pancakes right about now."

Alice yipped—that's the only word for it; she sounded like a baby coyote—and threw a piece of toast at him. Hard. It hit him on the shoulder and bounced onto the table.

"Dude, what is your problem?" he complained. "I didn't do anything. Well, I slept in, but since when is that a crime? And it looks like you guys figured it out." He picked up a knife and spread peanut butter on his toast. "Tasty," he said. "Is there coffee? I need me some java." He winked at Alice, and she looked as if she was going to have a seizure.

"That's enough, kids," Rahim said. He turned to Chad. "Tara is missing, Chad, and everyone is understandably upset." Then he looked around at the rest of us. "Being anxious and frightened is normal in a situation like this, but let's try to stay calm. Anxiety is directly related to your self-talk, so try to be aware of your thoughts. This is an opportunity to practice new ways of coping. So—circle time."

He pulled out a chair and sat down, gesturing to the rest of us to leave the mess of dishes and move into the group area. His authority should have been seriously undercut by the *Kiss the Cook* apron he was wearing, but soon everyone, even Chad, was sitting in a circle. Claire was gone. Maybe that helped. Maybe she was doing the right thing and calling the cops, but I doubted it. She and Warren were probably searching our cabins, looking for clues—or, just as likely, looking for something they could use to shift the blame to us and cover their own asses. A joint, which they'd find easily enough in Chad's stuff. A condom. A bottle. Some pills. A journal. A sketchbook like mine. Which she would never find.

ELEVEN

Alice

I had this awful gut-sinking feeling about Tara. Maybe it was because of the way Caleb had guessed that Tara was suicidal, way back before we even got to the island. Or maybe it was because of how totally messed up and sad Tara had been in group the day before, when she talked about Noah.

Those scars on her arms didn't exactly shout resilience.

Or maybe they did. Maybe that was exactly what they represented. Maybe those scars were evidence of how she'd managed to survive whatever crap had happened in her life.

Still, no matter how you looked at it, there was something fragile about Tara.

Rahim had us all in a circle, talking. *Processing what has happened,* he said, which made no sense because we had no clue what actually had.

I let the voices wash over me. *Blah, blah, blah.* It was mostly Imogen and Mandy doing the talking. And Rahim, of course. None of the guys had much to say. I sure didn't. I couldn't even stand listening. Because I'd heard something during the night, and I hadn't bothered to sit up, let alone check if everything was okay. I'd just rolled over and gone back to sleep.

It could've been anything—a tree branch falling, a door banging in the wind. Only now I wondered if it was Tara leaving the cabin to go…well, to go do whatever it was she had done.

Beside me, Mandy crossed her legs. "I can't even *imagine* how I'd deal if someone I loved threw themselves in front of a train."

"Jesus Christ." Caleb stood up so abruptly that his chair fell over backward with a crash. "This is so messed up. Why are we just sitting here when someone is missing?"

"Warren is out on the water. He's going to circumnavigate the island," Rahim reminded us. "And Claire is rechecking the buildings."

"I'm going to help look," Caleb said.

"Me too," I said, jumping to my feet.

"I'll come with you," Nick said.

Rahim let out a sigh. "You're all worried, and you feel a need to take action—"

"Yes! Which is what *you* should be doing!" I said. Yelled, really. My voice just came out that way. "Why the hell hasn't anyone called the police? Or, I don't know, someone official. Someone who can get a proper search party together."

"Yeah," Jason put in. "Even if you don't give two shits about Tara, you'd think you'd be covering your own asses here. You're going to get the pants sued off you. Don't you have some kind of emergency plan?"

Rahim blinked rapidly and ran his fingers through his hair. "Look, let's give it a little longer. If Warren comes back and he hasn't found her, I'll talk to him and Claire and suggest that we use the radio to call for outside help." He wiped his hands on his shorts. "In the meantime, let's pair up and check around the camp again."

I wanted to get out the door before he could change his mind. But once we were outside, we stood around staring at each other in the cool damp air. The thing was, we were on an island. A small island at that. There weren't a lot of places Tara could be hiding, and they'd already all been checked. And a kayak was gone, so obviously she'd taken it…

I clenched my hands into fists.

It didn't make any sense. I mean, I wanted to get the hell out of here myself, but no way would I attempt to get to the mainland in a kayak. And I was a strong swimmer, and in good shape. Tara was scared of water. And she wasn't stupid.

If Tara had left in that boat, it wasn't an escape attempt. It was suicide. But I couldn't see her doing it either way.

I heard footsteps. Someone was coming around the corner, heading up on the path from the water. I caught my breath.

But it wasn't Tara. "What are you all doing?" Claire demanded. "Where's Rahim?"

"We're going to search again," Caleb said. "In case we missed something."

"And then Rahim's going to call for help," I added. "I mean, if Warren doesn't find her..."

Claire was pale and sweating, her eyes pink-rimmed. "I just saw Warren—"

"He didn't find her," I cut in. "I knew he wouldn't."

She narrowed her eyes suspiciously. "What do you mean, you *knew*?"

"What is wrong with you people?" I wanted to grab Claire and shake her, hard. "There's no way Tara would take off in a boat. She hates the water. And she's scared of drowning. Even if she wanted to...even if she was...she wouldn't do it like that. Pills maybe. But risk drowning? Not a chance."

Claire shook her head. She was trying to hide it, but she looked scared, and I realized again that she really wasn't that much older than the rest of us. "I'm on my way to call for help," she said. "I want you all to go back to your cabins and try to rest." She jogged off toward the mess hall.

"Yeah, a nap sounds sweet," Chad said and headed in the direction of the guys' cabin.

Caleb looked pissed. "I'm going to look in the woods again," he said. Jason and Nick offered to go with him, and they took off. I figured they were avoiding Chad as much as looking for Tara. Not that I blamed them. I'd rather have poked myself in the eye with a sharp stick than shared a cabin with that asshole.

Mandy took off, heading back to our cabin. "Guess I better follow her," Imogen said, hanging back and sounding reluctant. "She's a wreck."

"Yeah," I said. "You go with her—we don't want to lose anyone else. I'm going to poke around a bit."

Imogen gave me an awkward shoulder punch. For some reason my cheeks felt warm, and I couldn't quite meet her eyes. "Um, so. I'll see you later," I said, and I took off sprinting down the path to the beach. It was quiet and empty and would have probably felt peaceful under different circumstances. As it was, my gut was churning and my head buzzing with questions. I sat on a huge, damp driftwood log, slipped off my hoodie and stuck it under my butt so I wouldn't get soaked. The red kayak was there, where Warren had pulled it up on the rocks above the high-tide line. You could see the indentations in the stones where the yellow kayak had been. The scene shifted in my mind, like camera lenses clicking into place, sharpening the focus.

What did I know? I'd heard a noise in the night. Maybe one o'clock, two o'clock? Something like that. Tara was missing. A kayak was gone...

There had to be clues here. My mother was a detective. And I was a *CSI* addict.

I walked over to the space where the second kayak had been and tried to imagine the scene. Tara, dressing silently and tiptoeing out of our cabin, walking down the path to the beach, looking out at the blackness of the sea. Pulling the kayak over the stones and across the sand, down to the edge of the water, standing there with the icy waves lapping at her feet. Rolling up her jeans to push the boat out...

But I didn't believe it. There had to be some other explanation.

There weren't any drag lines on the sand to show where the kayak had been pulled to the edge of the water— I guessed the tide must already have come and gone, wiping the rocky beach clean. I looked back up to where the rocks ran into a dirt bank, then at the scrubby grass and trees above.

Nothing. Just rocks and mud and—

A footprint. Right at the edge of the beach, where the rocks thinned out and bared the muddy ground beneath, was one almost perfect footprint.

I almost laughed. A footprint was a classic clue in the movies, but what did it actually mean? That someone had stepped on the dirt bank above the beach? Big deal. It could have been any one of us, launching our stupid paper boats the day before.

Only…it had been raining last night, hadn't it? It had started drizzling just as we finished up the ritual, and it had poured while we ate dinner, a heavy patter-patter on the roof of the mess hall. It hadn't stopped until after we were in bed. So someone had been on the beach later than that. Maybe this footprint wasn't nothing after all.

I crossed the rocks, stepping carefully over the jumble of driftwood that crisscrossed the beach, and stopped a couple of feet away from the footprint. It was obviously made by someone with bigger feet than mine, which basically narrowed it down to everyone else on the island. I balanced on one foot, slipped my other foot out of its muddy runner and held the shoe above the footprint. Bigger by several inches, so probably not one of the girls. And it looked like a boot with a heavy tread.

I'd noticed that Warren wore Kodiaks. He'd been down here this morning, getting the kayak. But it could just as easily be from any of the other guys. I was pretty sure I'd seen Caleb in hiking boots, and maybe Jason too. I'd have to find some way of visiting the guys' cabin to check out their footwear and shoe sizes. And Rahim too—he was a socks-and-sandals guy, but he probably had brand-new Gore-Tex hiking boots to go with his brand-new *Canadian Outdoorsman* wardrobe.

Maybe Tara had been meeting one of the guys for some reason. It didn't seem likely, but it made more sense than her sneaking down here in the middle of the night to go kayaking in the dark.

I backed away from the footprint. I wished I had my phone so I could take a photo. I should protect the print somehow, I thought, in case it was evidence. Evidence of what, I had no idea, but I grabbed a few sticks and built a sort of tepee over the footprint, as if I was making a bonfire or something. Hmm. That would protect the footprint from being stepped on, but not from rain or high tides...

I was being an idiot.

I turned and began walking back to the path, past the big driftwood log I'd been sitting on. My hoodie was still lying on the log, and I bent to pick it up.

And right by where I'd been sitting on the log, just behind where my legs had been minutes earlier, was a dark, reddish stain.

I swallowed. Stared. Dropped to my knees and looked at the stain more closely.

Could it actually be *blood*?

Or was I being completely crazy? I mean, I decide to treat the beach like a crime scene, and next thing you know I'm seeing footprints and bloodstains everywhere? *Yeah. Get a grip, Alice.*

The dark patch was a couple of inches wide and ran down the side of the log in a thick dark streak. It sure looked like blood. But it could've been…I didn't know. Something else. I just couldn't think what.

I stood up, wrapped my arms around myself and shivered.

Then the gong sounded—loudly and urgently—five times. Emergency meeting. I grabbed my hoodie and ran to join the others.

TWELVE
Alice

Rahim and Claire were waiting for us, the chairs still arranged in a circle. People took their seats. I glanced around the room, first at the faces—everyone looked anxious, eager for news—and then at the feet.

Caleb's feet were massive, not surprisingly—he must've been at least six foot four—and he was wearing hiking boots. So were Jason and Chad. Rahim was wearing his Keen sandals with gray socks, and Nick was wearing Converse high-tops.

Not that this proved anything.

"I'm afraid we've got some bad news," Claire said. Her hair was pulled back into a ponytail, and she was nervously twisting a loose strand between her fingers.

"Oh my god." Beside me, Imogen gasped, and her hand flew to her mouth. "Tara. Did she kill herself? Did you find her body?"

Rahim put a hand on Imogen's arm. "No, no. Nothing like that. It's the radio."

Claire nodded. "The radio's not working. I tried to call the coast guard, but it seems to be completely dead."

"*Dead*. Nice word choice," Imogen whispered to me.

Jason spoke up. "I'm pretty good with electronics. I can take a look."

Claire frowned slightly. "Well, let's wait until Warren gets back. He may be able to get it working. No offense, Jason. I just don't want to risk having you take it apart and make things worse."

Jason folded his arms across his chest, clearly annoyed. "I'm not going to make things worse. I know what I'm doing."

"I'm sure you do, Jason," Claire said. "And if Warren can't get it working, we'll take you up on that offer. But let's wait for him."

"Good idea," Rahim chimed in. "And in the meantime, let's pick up where we left off and take some time to focus on how we are all feeling."

Not surprisingly, the group session was a dismal failure. Rahim rambled on about shock and trauma and assured us about a hundred times that whatever we were feeling was normal. Nobody wanted to discuss their feelings though.

Claire looked pale and tense. "I'll start," she offered. "I'm feeling…well, I'm devastated that a camper has gone missing on my watch."

A camper. Not Tara, just *a camper*. I figured she was probably envisioning a future that included her INTRO business getting some seriously bad press, and maybe a lawsuit or two. She squeezed out a few tears, but honestly, I couldn't shake the conviction that she was more worried about her business than about Tara herself.

I was almost certain that Caleb was the only one with feet that big, but I wished I'd measured the footprint. My mom would've thought of that for sure. And I kept picturing that stain-that-was-possibly-blood on the log.

I wanted to talk to someone about what I'd seen, but it was scary, and I wasn't sure who I could trust. Imogen, maybe? I liked her, but I wasn't sure how truthful she was—some of her stories were hard to believe. Still, I couldn't imagine that she had anything to do with Tara's disappearance.

Soon Warren reappeared, grim-faced. He shook his head wordlessly, and Mandy let out a sob. Claire jumped to her feet and clutched Warren's arm like it was a life preserver. The two of them rushed off together, presumably to fix the radio.

I hoped to hell they could get it working. I guessed if they couldn't, Warren would have to paddle the kayak back to the mainland to get help. I assumed that was possible. After all, people kayaked all around the Gulf Islands, right? And Warren was fit enough if anyone was. It'd mean another delay though. There should have been a search-and-rescue operation happening before we'd even had breakfast. Instead, it was practically dinnertime and still no action. Jason was right—Claire and Warren might be hoping to avoid bad publicity, but they were pretty much begging for a lawsuit. Why didn't they have a backup plan? A second emergency radio or flares or something. Weren't there any standards they had to meet? This was crazy.

I felt another flash of anger toward my mother. What the hell had she been thinking, sending me here?

Rahim cleared his throat. "Well. It's understandable that everyone is a little overwhelmed—"

"Can you *please* stop saying everything is understandable?" Imogen snarled.

"Oh my god," Mandy said. "Oh my god. What if Tara's dead? What if her body is, like, lying somewhere in the woods?"

"Mandy, take a deep breath and stop catastrophizing," Rahim said.

Mandy looked shocked, but she took a great gulp of air.

"Good," Rahim said. "And another." He glanced around the circle. "Look, let's get dinner started. Never mind what the schedule says. Chad and Caleb, can you clear up the mess from lunch and maybe do some dishes? Imogen and Alice, how about you two chop up some veggies for a salad. Jason, you're in charge of pasta. Mandy and Nick..." He looked around. "Uh, dessert? Cookies? Whatever you can come up with, okay?"

Mandy took another noisy gulp of air and nodded. "I make the best peanut-butter cookies," she said. "Seriously. They're to die for."

Imogen caught my eye. "I hope not," she whispered, and I almost snorted.

We found a clear patch of counter close to the sink. Imogen washed red peppers and mushrooms and passed them to me to chop. I looked around. The kitchen was pretty large, but with this many people crowded into it, I didn't want to bring up the blood on the beach.

"That was smart, didn't you think?" Imogen handed me a tomato.

"What was?"

"Rahim. Giving everyone something to do."

I looked up at her in surprise. "I guess."

"Mandy was starting to do that thing she does, you know, hyperventilating, flapping her hands. About to go into full-on panic mode…" Imogen pointed at her with a cucumber. "Look at her now."

I looked. Mandy was hanging on to Nick's arm, giggling and whispering something. "Huh."

"And he put her with Nick too." She nodded for emphasis. "That Rahim? He comes across as a bit goofy, but he's not stupid. He's hiding a sharp mind behind all that psychobabble."

"What?" She'd lost me. "Why would Rahim hide anything? And why's it good that Mandy's with Nick? You mean because her flirting won't go anywhere?"

She shook her head. "Nick's good with people. Likes taking care of them. He wants to be a nurse, you know?"

"No. I didn't." It was like we'd been on different islands. "How do you know all this?"

She laughed. "I just pay attention."

SARAH N. HARVEY & ROBIN STEVENSON

"I pay attention," I said, slicing a mushroom. *Thwack, thwack, thwack.*

"You're always off in your head, thinking about something." Imogen put her hand on my wrist. "Hey. Don't be mad. It's not a bad thing."

Even after the salad was ready, I could still feel the warmth on my wrist where she had touched me.

*   *   *

There was no way I could get to sleep that night. Warren hadn't been able to get the radio working, and he hadn't let Jason try, which made no sense. I couldn't believe we were stuck here, having to go on with this farce of a program, and still there was no one doing a proper search for Tara. I lay in my narrow bed under the scratchy INTRO blanket, and a tear leaked out of my eye. Thank God for pitch-darkness.

Imogen and Mandy chatted for a while. It was mostly Mandy talking and Imogen listening, and of course it was about the guys. They both thought Caleb was cute, and Mandy thought Jason was all right too. "He's actually really shy," she said. "You wouldn't think it, because he comes across as cocky, right? But one on one, when you talk to him? He's not like that at all." I could hear her rolling over in the dark. "He's sweet."

And so on. *Blah, blah, blah.* I wasn't in the mood for gossip and small talk. Still, listening to them made me feel even more alone. I was desperate to tell someone about the footprint and the blood, but I hadn't been able to get Imogen alone. I considered telling them both. I couldn't imagine Mandy having anything to do with Tara's disappearance, but if I mentioned blood, she'd probably lose it completely. Better not to risk it.

They finally fell quiet, but I was wide awake with my thoughts buzzing around. I kept going over my first night here—how I'd sat on the end of Tara's bed and we'd talked. Not about anything important—just about her liking cooking and about Caleb's artwork. It didn't seem like the sort of conversation someone would have if they were planning to kill themselves.

"Are you still awake?" I whispered. "Imogen? Mandy?"

No one answered.

I got out of bed, padded barefoot across the wooden floor and sat on Tara's bed again. It was still unmade, the way she'd left it.

There was this ache in my chest. I wanted so incredibly much to talk to my mom. Yeah, I was pissed off that she'd made me come here, but I got it. I really did. If I ever had a kid who was royally screwing up in potentially fatal ways, I'd probably do something drastic too.

I sent telepathic messages across the ocean and through the city streets to our condo, concentrating as hard as I could. I didn't really believe in that kind of thing, but I wished with all my heart I did. If my mom would only walk in right now, I'd throw myself into her arms and give her the biggest all-is-forgiven hug ever.

I lay down on the bed with my head on Tara's pillow. I thought I could smell the faintest hint of her shampoo on the bedding, but maybe I was imagining it. As I curled up on my side, something crinkled under the sheet. I slid my hand beneath the covers and felt around.

A scrap of paper.

I tiptoed back to my own bed, grabbed my flashlight from under my pillow and burrowed under my blanket before switching it on.

In my hand was a small sheet of lined paper that looked like it'd been torn from a notebook. On it, in tidy, slanting all caps:

MEET ME ON THE BEACH TONIGHT AFTER THE OTHERS ARE ASLEEP

—CALEB

My heart sank. I wasn't sure why, but I really didn't want it to be Caleb.

He's pretty cute, Tara had said. And she'd gone on about how nice and sincere he was…

I pictured those supersized hiking boots. And he always had a notebook with him. He tried to hide it, like he was embarrassed about writing in a journal or something, but I'd seen it sticking out of his hoodie pocket. It looked about the same size as this note.

Had Tara met Caleb on the beach the night before? And what happened? Did they have a fight? Was that why she'd taken off? I pictured the blood on the log again. Had Caleb done something to her? Hurt her somehow?

I couldn't see it, but you can't really tell about people. Mom's always saying how charming sociopaths can be.

Or—what if Tara was cutting again? That would explain the blood. Maybe Caleb had tried to stop her. But if that was the case, why wouldn't he tell the truth about it?

Even if he hadn't killed her, he was obviously hiding something.

TUESDAY

THIRTEEN
Caleb

Twenty-four hours after Tara had gone missing, I was back in the mess hall, poking at the breakfast Mandy and Nick had prepared for us—oatmeal with raisins. I hate raisins and I'm not keen on oatmeal, but I was hungry, so I picked out the raisins, loaded the oatmeal with brown sugar and flooded it with milk. Alice and I were on lunch duty—maybe I'd be able to find something tasty in the fridge. Like a cheeseburger and some fries. Somehow I doubted it.

Imogen and Alice were sitting together, chatting in low voices—I had a feeling they were talking about me, because every so often they sent dark looks in my direction before returning to their whisper fest. Jason was slumped over at one of the tables, his head resting on his arms, an empty bowl beside him. Chad was nowhere to be seen, which was weird because he'd left the cabin before me. No sign of any of the counselors either. Maybe they were off somewhere staring at the broken radio and deciding how exactly to handle the inevitable lawsuits...

I had no idea what the hell was going on.

Mandy slid into the chair beside me with a dramatic sigh and slipped off an apron embroidered with the INTRO logo, revealing white short-shorts, a hot-pink tank top and a lot of cleavage. I averted my eyes, disgusted with myself for noticing this under the present circumstances.

"Sorry about the oatmeal," Mandy said. "Looks like barf, right? Cooking's so not my thing—I'm the queen of takeout—and Nick isn't much better. I thought all gay guys were totally into gourmet cooking and home decor and fashion and shit. Obviously I was wrong. Although I guess there's not much you can do with crap ingredients. Even I know that instant oatmeal is gross. And this coffee?" She held up her mug. "The worst. They sure aren't spending our parents' money on quality food and beverages. First place I hit when we get back to town will be a Starbucks."

I looked down at the bowl in front of me. "Better than starving," I said. "Long time till lunch." I figured she was chattering away mindlessly because she was stressed and anxious—anything to fill the silence—but it was still annoying.

She stretched her arms over her head and yawned. I could see a tattoo on her right boob.

She caught me looking and giggled. "It's Chinese for 'beautiful spirit.' I got it when I was thirteen. I talked some random old guy into coming to the tattoo place with me

and pretending to be my dad. I can be very persuasive."
She winked at me. "My real dad flipped out, but what could
he do? Pay for me to get the tatt lasered off?"

What was there to say, really? *You're an idiot. Your tattoo
probably means "dumb chicken."* I kept shoveling oatmeal into
my mouth, hoping she would get bored and go away.

Chad finally slouched into the mess hall, scratching his
balls and yawning. Maybe Mandy would recognize her soul
mate and leave me the hell alone.

No such luck.

She took a sip of her coffee, grimaced and said, "What do
you think happened to Tara? It totally creeps me out. I don't
think I slept at all last night. I mean, are we safe? Especially
the girls. What if there's, like, a killer hiding on the island?
Unless she really did kill herself, and then we're fine, right?"

I was saved from answering her by Rahim, who had
turned up in the mess hall looking like shit. What little hair
he had was uncombed, and he appeared to have slept in his
clothes.

Alice and Imogen leaped up and peppered him with
questions. "Did you find her? Is she okay? Have you called
for help? Are we going home?"

This last question was from Alice, who truly looked as
if she hadn't slept. Her face was pasty, and her lips looked
chapped and swollen, as if she had been chewing on them
all night.

"Going home?" Rahim sounded surprised. "Claire and
Warren haven't said anything to me about that. Right now

our focus is on Tara." He held up a hand as if to ward off more questions. "The radio seems to be a lost cause, so we don't actually have any way of calling for help."

"Shouldn't Warren take the other kayak and paddle somewhere?" Alice said. "There are lots of other islands around. And boats. I mean, I've seen sailboats going by, and I bet they have radios on them. And flares." She scowled. "Some people actually prepare for emergencies, you know."

Rahim hesitated. "Um. Well, that is a good idea, Alice. I did make a similar suggestion to Claire and Warren, but they…well. They're checking the island again, in case we missed something."

They were putting off the inevitable, I thought, but the delay in getting help was only going to blow up in their faces.

"Missed something?" Imogen's voice was a squeak. "Like a body?"

"We're still hopeful that she made it to safety in the kayak." Rahim's voice shook a bit.

Alice made another one of her odd animal noises. This one probably meant *How can you people be so stupid?*

Rahim ignored her. "All we can do now is support each other and look after ourselves—"

"*Look after ourselves?*" Mandy's eyes widened. "You mean, like, protect ourselves from a killer?"

"I understand that you're worried and afraid, Mandy," Rahim said, "and I'm here to help you process your emotions, but we don't have any reason to believe Tara is dead. As soon as there's any news, Claire and Warren will let us know. In the meantime, let's get out in the sunshine. Bring a coffee or some juice, if you want, and meet me on the beach."

He poured some coffee into his travel mug (*Imagine. Believe. Achieve. Ravenspirit Retreat, 2007*) and walked out of the room, his shoulders slumped. I caught Jason's eye, and he shrugged.

"You heard the man," I said. "Let's go process some emotions, people."

"But put your dishes in the sink to soak first, you effing donkeys!" Nick yelled from the kitchen in a pretty good Gordon Ramsay imitation. "Oatmeal's a bitch if it dries out."

"Yes, chef!" Jason said. Everyone laughed. Nervous laughter but better than nothing. It was unsettling to hear Nick freak out, even if it was a joke. Though I was starting to think that maybe no one was what they seemed. Maybe Nick was one of those quiet psychos who lull you into feeling safe and then slip poison in your oatmeal.

He stayed in character, screaming, "Do you want a bloody medal?" when I slid my dish into the sink.

When I glared at him, he flushed and said, "Too much?" in his normal voice.

"Nah. I'm just a bit jumpy, that's all," I said. I was worse than jumpy—I was getting totally paranoid. And Alice kept looking at me with her eyes narrowed and her mouth a hard, straight line, totally pissed off and suspicious, which didn't help. What was her problem? I hadn't done anything to her.

"I hear ya," Nick replied. "Whole thing is nuts. And now we have to talk about how we feel? I'd rather scrub oatmeal crust off these dishes, man."

I stayed and helped Nick clean up, and then we headed down to the beach together. You could already see how people were aligning themselves. Imogen and Alice were sitting with their backs against a log, pitching stones into the water and speaking in near whispers. Chad and Mandy were huddled together on a large rock. Mandy was giggling and stroking Chad's biceps (which weren't anywhere near as impressive as Warren's). Jason waved Nick and me over to the log he was sitting on. I wondered where Tara would have fit in. From what little she had told us, I guessed she had a hard time fitting in anywhere. Maybe that was why her boyfriend's suicide had hit her so hard. Maybe he was all she had.

Rahim was sitting on a large rock, facing out to sea, his travel mug balanced beside him. Chad picked up a stone and nailed the travel mug, which wobbled and then rolled off the rock and into the water. When Rahim startled and turned around, I wondered if he'd been crying. I couldn't be sure— his glasses were all smudged.

"Dude, everybody's here," Chad said. "Let the processing begin."

"Shut up, Chad," Alice said. "You're such an asshole." She got up and fished Rahim's travel mug out of the water with a piece of driftwood.

Rahim clambered down from the rock, took the mug from her and wiped it on his sweater. "Thank you, Alice."

He took a sip from his mug and made a face—maybe his coffee was a little salty. "Perhaps the easiest thing would be for us to use a talking stick." He picked up the piece of driftwood Alice had used to fish out his mug. "Do you all know how a talking stick works?"

"Person who holds it talks. No interruptions," Jason said. "My mom's grandma was First Nations. We used one in our family if there was some big issue to discuss, like whether we should let our sister join the family business. It didn't always work out that well though. Josh, my oldest brother, got a concussion when our da clubbed him on the head with the talking stick." Jason laughed, like this was actually a funny anecdote and not his life. Or maybe he was making sure none of us dared feel sorry for him. He folded his arms across his chest. "Our da's Irish, and a drunk. Stereotype, but there you have it. He thought the talking stick was bullshit."

Rahim ground the talking stick into the pebbles. "And what do you think?" he asked Jason. "Is it bullshit?"

Jason shrugged. "Not really. It meant that for once my sister didn't get drowned out by her brothers and our da."

"And did she get to join the family business?" Imogen asked.

"She did," Jason said. "That girl could get in and out of a house faster than any of us. But she quit after a couple of years. She's studying to be a lawyer." He laughed. "The last time the family used the talking stick was when she announced she was going straight. That was quite the night. The talking stick ended up as kindling. Da wasn't keen on what Shannon had to say about her new career. He thinks lawyers are—what's the word?— shysters. No daughter of mine blah, blah, blah. He's proud of his sons, though, even if we are convicted felons."

There was a long silence, and Jason's final words hung in the air. *Convicted felons.* I felt like I should say something, but I couldn't think what.

Finally Rahim turned to the rest of us. "So who would like to start?" he asked. When no one volunteered, he thumped the stick on a rock. "Okay, I'll go first. I am worried about Tara and afraid that she has harmed herself. I am also ashamed that I didn't do anything to help her. That I didn't comprehend the depth of her despair."

I was glad when he stopped talking. The last thing we needed was to have to worry about Rahim's state of mind.

Rahim handed the stick to Alice, still looking upset. She studied it and then tossed it to Imogen, who stood up, took a deep breath and said, "I don't know what to say. I mean, I hardly knew her. She seemed super unhappy but not, you know, suicidal or anything. We talked on the Zodiac a bit, before I started puking. And she said she and her gran went through a lot together when Tara's grandpa died. She took care of her gran, you know? I can't believe she'd intentionally cause her more pain." She passed the stick to Mandy and sat down. Alice put her arms around Imogen, who buried her face in Alice's shoulder. Those two sure seemed to be bonding over this.

Mandy dropped the stick as if it were a poisonous snake. "This is totally freaking me out, you guys. I just want to get off this island in one piece." She turned to Chad. "You take it."

Chad grabbed the stick from her. "Let's get real. We only met Tara a couple of days ago. It's not like she meant anything to any of us. I thought she was a drag. But I hope she's alive."

I wondered if he was telling the truth. He had left our cabin that first night. Who knew what he had been doing. Maybe he and Tara had met, and things had gone sideways. Unhappy girl hooks up with total jerk. Hard to imagine any girl being interested in Chad, but I guessed it was possible.

Chad threw the stick to me javelin style. I caught it in one hand and twirled it like a drum major in a parade. I considered whacking him with it but decided not to make things worse.

"Wow, you got some mad skills there, bro," Chad said. "Learn that from the cheerleaders on your football team?"

"Shut up, Chad," I said. "You had your chance to speak. Now it's mine."

FOURTEEN
Caleb

The stick was smooth, as if it had been sanded by the wind and the waves, and there was a knot on it that looked like a face. If I'd been alone, I would have drawn it. I would have drawn lots of things—the way Alice's shoes were almost buried in pebbles, the strange little driftwood shelter someone had made by one of the logs, the tangle of purple beach peas that swarmed over the bushes above the beach. But drawing would have to wait.

"I don't have any theories about what's happened to Tara," I said. "I hope she took a kayak and got picked up by a passing fishing boat. And I can understand why she'd do that. Try to get away, I mean. But we need to contact the coast guard or the police, even if it means figuring out how to use the radio ourselves. I don't believe Claire and Warren are going to contact anyone. They don't want the authorities to know what's going on. Bad for their business. I bet they're hoping Tara will turn up safe and sound and we'll carry on as if nothing has happened, but that's pretty messed up, and it's dangerous. Someone's life is at stake here. They don't know what they're doing and—sorry, Rahim, but you don't seem to either." I wondered if Rahim would challenge me, but all he did was nod.

I passed the stick to Jason, who pointed at me and said, "What he said" and then walked the stick over to Alice.

She took it this time but stayed seated, one arm still around Imogen.

"Caleb's right," she said, not looking at me. "We need to call for help." She put the stick down. "Anybody want to volunteer to talk to Claire with me?"

"I'll do it," Chad said. "But maybe Caleb should come too, in case Claire needs some convincing."

"*Convincing?*" I stood up, and my voice came out louder and angrier than I meant it to. "What's that supposed to mean? Because I beat up my stepdad I'm your go-to guy for intimidating people? Weren't you listening yesterday? I only hit guys who are hurting someone I care about. Take Jason if you need backup. And stay away from me from now on. My anger-management program doesn't seem to be working."

"Now, boys," Rahim said, getting to his feet and waving his coffee mug at us. "There's no need for that kind of talk. It won't help matters. Caleb, you and Alice are on lunch duty."

That was going to be fun, I thought. All morning Alice had been avoiding me—and now she and Imogen were looking at me like I'd just murdered a litter of kittens.

"I'll help in the kitchen," Imogen said.

Rahim nodded. "Nick and Mandy, would you like to stay here and do a sitting meditation with me? I find that really helpful when I'm stressed." He patted the rock next to him.

To my surprise, Nick nodded. He and Mandy climbed up onto the rock, where they assumed the lotus position beside Rahim. Nick looked away as I passed him—sheepishly, I thought. Mandy already had her eyes closed.

Alice and Imogen and I made lunch in silence—lentil soup from a vat in the fridge and grilled cheese sandwiches. Oatmeal-raisin cookies for dessert. Just as Imogen was about to hit the gong, Chad stormed into the room, yelling, "I could have fixed it, man." Jason followed behind, a look of irritation on his face.

"What's going on?" I asked.

"We couldn't find Claire or Warren, and the goddamn radio's broken," Chad said. "If Captain Klepto here hadn't got in my way, I coulda fixed it and we'd be outta here." He flung himself down in a chair and started stuffing his face with cookies.

"That true?" I asked Jason.

He shook his head. "No way Chad or anyone else could fix that radio."

"Why not?" Alice asked.

"Because there's a part missing—an important part. Without it, the radio's toast."

"And you know this how?" Chad asked, his mouth full of cookie. "Did you fix electronics as well as steal them?"

"Pretty much," Jason said. "I've always liked taking things apart, figuring out how they work. Toasters, blenders, stereos—you name it, I can fix it."

"So we're stuck here," Imogen said, her voice quivering. "Until Saturday, when the boat comes back. That's four days."

"But hey," Chad said, "if a small appliance breaks, we're in great shape."

"Shut your cakehole," Jason said, but he sounded more tired than angry. Me, I was the opposite. No radio. No boat. A missing girl and a lot of unanswered questions.

And nobody was doing anything about it.

"Maybe Tara's disappearance was no accident," Alice said. "Maybe the radio was sabotaged. Maybe—"

She was interrupted by Warren, who strode into the mess hall, rubbing his massive paws together. "What's for lunch, kids?" he asked. "I'm hungry as a bear after a long winter." As if nothing was wrong. As if Tara wasn't missing and the radio wasn't toast and his wife wasn't the crappiest therapist on the planet.

As if we weren't all getting really scared.

Everybody stared at Warren as if we had been turned to stone. When Claire and Rahim appeared in the doorway, the spell was broken. Everyone but Alice and me pressed around the three adults, peppering them with questions.

Warren held up one meaty hand. "Settle down, people. All in good time."

"Good time?" Imogen said. "What does that mean? Have you found Tara?"

"No," Claire said. "But there's no need to panic." She looked directly at Mandy, who was starting to whimper.

"We're not panicking," Imogen said. "We're asking questions. Like, is there some kind of plan? Have you called for help?"

Claire folded her arms across her chest. "There's no reason to believe any of you are in danger. As I said before, we are following procedure."

I ladled soup into bowls while Alice cut up the sandwiches and piled them on plates. Nobody was saying anything new. Nobody had any answers. And Mandy's whimpering had escalated to full-on wailing.

"Lunch is ready," I yelled. "Get it while it's hot."

Claire was the first to break free of the group. "Warren is going to head out in the kayak this afternoon. He's bound to run into another boat sooner or later. He can use their radio to call for help. Right now we need some fuel to keep our strength up. That path across the island isn't going to build itself."

FIFTEEN

Alice

I had zero appetite. The soup smelled vile, and I couldn't imagine eating. Even the thought made me want to puke.

All I could think about was the note from Caleb I'd found in Tara's bed. I'd told Imogen about it—and about the footprint and the blood on the beach too—and we'd talked it over endlessly. We couldn't decide what to do. I thought we should confront him directly, but Imogen thought that was too dangerous—what if he freaked out? Then we wondered if maybe we should tell one of the adults—but at this point, neither of us really trusted them to handle things. Perhaps the safest thing was to lie low and keep our mouths shut until we could get out of here. We had gone around in circles and still hadn't made a decision. I could barely bring myself to look at Caleb. I couldn't believe I'd had to make lunch with him. At least Imogen had stayed with me the whole time.

I pulled my feet up in front of me on the hard wooden chair, wrapped my arms around my knees and sat there, watching everyone else eat: Warren shoveling soup into his mouth, Claire taking a delicate bite from her sandwich, Rahim fussily picking the green onions out of his bowl. Chad belched loudly. That guy was everything I despised wrapped up in one ugly package. I stood up. My heart was pounding like I'd sprinted a mile. Pounding so hard it felt like it was trying to get out.

What the *hell* was wrong with these people?

Imogen turned around in her chair and looked at me. "Hey. Alice."

To my horror, my eyes seemed to be leaking. What the hell? I *never* cried in front of other people—I'd had a show-no-weakness motto since I was a little kid. I swiped my hand across my eyes roughly. "Sorry."

"It's okay. This is totally messed up."

I looked down at her dark brown eyes, her glossy red lips. Her chin was lifted in her usual defiant don't-mess-with-me pose, but she was reaching a hand toward me. "I have to get out of here," I said.

"Want me to come with you?" She pushed her chair back.

I hesitated. I wanted to be alone, but I didn't feel safe. We had no idea what had happened to Tara. We were trapped on this island. And ever since I'd seen the blood on the log, I couldn't get the image out of my mind.

"Yeah," I told her, taking her outstretched hand in mine. Her nails were painted black and bitten to the quick. "Come with me."

We were walking toward the door when Rahim spotted us. "Where are you two going?"

Chad wolf-whistled. "Gonna get some *action*, girls? Can I watch?"

Imogen's hand was still in mine, but I didn't let go. "Some of us actually give a shit about Tara, asshole. Some of us, believe it or not, have a little more on our minds."

"Yeah. Plus, even if we *were* hooking up, just thinking about you would be enough to put me off," Imogen said.

"Ooh," Chad said. "That hurts."

Claire put down her sandwich. "Everyone stays with the group. This is a therapy program, not some do-whatever-the-hell-you-want, all-inclusive resort."

Imogen pulled her hand out of mine and whirled around to face Claire and the others. "It's been really therapeutic so far," she snapped. "I mean, I know I'm feeling better already. How about you guys?"

"Oh yeah," Nick said. "Feeling more heterosexual every day. Though that could just be Chad's presence. An excellent point you made there, Imogen. Chad could be like a poster child for aversion therapy. My parents would probably be all over it. A week with Chad and anyone would swear off guys for life."

"Oh my god! Aversion therapy? Is that a thing?" Mandy asked.

"It was a joke, Mandy," Nick said. "Ha-effing-ha."

"Okay, that's enough," Claire ordered. "There's no need to be—"

"No need to be worried?" My voice came out in a squeak. I forced it down an octave. "Shit scared? Freaking out? Tara is missing and may be dead, the radio is broken, we're trapped on an island in the middle of nowhere. Yeah. Nothing to worry about there."

"As Claire said, Warren's going to take a kayak out this afternoon," Rahim chimed in. "Right, Warren?"

There was a long silence, and people turned to look at Warren. He was sitting at the table, staring into his empty soup bowl.

"Warren," Claire said. "Are you okay?"

"Sorry, I…" He yawned. "What did you say?"

"Rahim was telling the group that you would be taking the kayak out…" Claire began.

Warren started to get to his feet, then sat back down. "Uh, I'm not feeling so great." He put his elbows on the table and held his head in his hands. "Dizzy."

"Maybe you should go lie down," Claire suggested, putting her hand on his arm.

"Maybe you should quit telling me what to do," Warren said, his words slurred.

Had he been *drinking*? Pretending to be out looking for Tara but secretly downing a few? Or more than a few by the sound of him. I wondered where his booze was stashed.

Claire looked like Warren had slapped her—frozen and shocked. Rahim got to his feet. "Come on," he said to Warren. "Take a break, huh? If you're not feeling well?"

"Stuff to do." Warren stood, took a step and staggered, off-balance.

Rahim grabbed his arm. It looked ridiculous—he was half Warren's size. "*I'll* get the kids working on the brush. Let's go, buddy."

We watched Rahim lead Warren out of the mess hall, with Claire trailing along behind. Warren was weaving along in a big S curve—he couldn't have passed the walk-a-straight-line test if his life depended on it—and it made me furious. I wanted the counselors, all three of them, to act like functioning adults. They were holding us captive here, and they needed to get us out of this mess.

SIXTEEN

Alice

Caleb and I cleared the table and did the dishes. He kept shooting me these puzzled, kicked-puppy looks, like he had no idea why I was doing my best to avoid him. By the time Claire and Rahim returned, everyone was sitting around talking in the same old circles: what could've happened to Tara, what were we going to do.

"Warren's lying down. He's feeling pretty sick," Rahim said, taking a seat at the table.

"What's wrong with him?" I asked. Not that they were going to admit Warren was drunk, but I wanted to see what kind of excuse they'd make.

"It looks like food poisoning," Claire said. There was a tiny pause while people took that in—and then everyone turned to look at me, Caleb and Imogen.

Caleb held his hands up. "Hey, not our fault! The soup was already made. All we did was heat it up and sprinkle a few green onions on top."

"Anyway, everyone ate it," I added. "Not just Warren."

"You didn't eat anything," Mandy pointed out.

I glared at her. "How would you know?"

"I was watching, because I thought you might have, like, an eating disorder or whatever. You didn't even taste the soup."

"Seriously, Mandy?" I was sick to death of people thinking I had an eating disorder just because I was kind of scrawny. "Here's a public service announcement for you: people actually come in different sizes. Fat, skinny, in between, whatever. Who cares."

"Sorr-eeee," she said, like she wasn't in the least.

"Anyway, you ate it, didn't you?" I pointed out. "And you're fine."

"Just a few mouthfuls. I didn't pig two bowls of it like Warren did," Mandy said. "It was gross."

"I hope we aren't all going to get sick," Rahim said to Claire. He'd lowered his voice, but it was still loud enough for us to hear.

"God." Claire ran her hands through her hair. "That's all we'd need."

Imogen stood up. "Can we not do the mass-hysteria thing, please? We don't even know that it's food poisoning. Personally, I thought Warren looked like he'd had a few drinks."

I turned to her gratefully. "That's what I thought."

"Warren has not been drinking," Claire said stiffly. "INTRO is a dry camp. Alice, alcohol is your issue, isn't it? And we know you have substance-abuse issues, Imogen. Don't you think it's possible that the two of you are projecting?"

"Alice made the lunch," Mandy said. "So of course *she* doesn't want to think it's food poisoning."

Rahim clapped his hands together. He'd picked up that habit from Claire, apparently. Like one person clapping at us wasn't annoying enough. "It's time to clear some brush," he said.

Twenty minutes later we were gathered outside the mess hall, dressed, as instructed, in long pants and long-sleeved shirts. The general idea was skin protection, but Mandy had her top three buttons undone, revealing the edge of a lacy bra, and the shirt knotted around her waist, baring a navel ring and several inches of tanned skin above her ultra-low-rise jeans.

Rahim was kitted out in one of those khaki vests with a gazillion pockets and zippers. He looked like he was all set for an African wilderness safari or something. There were a couple of cardboard boxes by his feet, and a pile of dangerous-looking implements. His forehead was shining with sweat.

I felt embarrassed for him. The brush-clearing mission was Warren's thing. I bet Rahim didn't have a clue what he was doing.

"All right!" he shouted. "Everyone ready to get started? Grab a pair of gloves from this box here…"

"Like we have a choice," Imogen muttered to me as we rummaged through the gloves. I kept pulling out left-handed ones. It was gross, sliding my hands into the damp rubber and wondering how many other people had worn them.

Rahim picked up an enormous pair of red-handled scissors and handed them to Jason. "We've got three sets of these, uh, these…"

"Pruning shears," Chad said.

We all stared at him.

"What?" He looked around the circle indignantly. "I had a summer job as groundskeeper at a golf course, okay?"

"Great!" Rahim said. "So a pair for you, then, and Jason and Mandy."

He bent down and picked up two machetes. "Caleb and Imogen, you two can take these."

Machetes? "Seriously?" I blurted. "Uh, I mean, is that really a good idea?"

Rahim looked at me, head tilted to one side like he had no idea what I meant.

Imogen and I exchanged glances. I didn't want to tell Rahim about the note—not here in front of everyone. I wasn't sure why. Maybe because, despite the evidence that he was hiding something, I still wasn't convinced Caleb was dangerous. On the other hand, maybe he was. I couldn't just let Rahim give him a weapon… "Um, Caleb is here because he assaulted someone," I said desperately. "And you're going to hand him a machete?"

"Because the guy was beating up my mother," Caleb said, taking the machete and scowling at me. "You think I should've stood back and let him hit her?"

"I didn't say that. But…" I trailed off. I didn't blame him for hitting the guy, but I couldn't exactly admit that now. I couldn't even imagine someone hitting my mother. Of course, she carried a gun. But I had a black belt in karate, and I wouldn't hesitate to use it if someone was hurting her.

"There were extenuating circumstances," Rahim said. "And I have the utmost faith in Caleb's ability to move on from that… incident."

Caleb looked at me. I couldn't meet his eyes. I swallowed hard, folded my arms across my chest and said nothing.

"And who's left…? Nick and Alice. Uh, how about you two take these hatchets?" Rahim held out two of the tiniest hatchets I'd ever seen. Not that I'd seen a lot of hatchets—the tools I was familiar with were more along the lines of food processors and coffee-bean grinders. These hatchets didn't look like they'd chop down anything much sturdier than a dandelion, and I couldn't help wondering why it was me and Nick who got them. I mean, the gay guy and the really small girl? Or was I being paranoid?

It really sucked how hard it was to tell sometimes.

Nick and I took the hatchets. I studied mine. It looked like a toy ax, or one of those bizarrely gendered tools—they might as well have made it pink and called it a Ladies' Hatchet.

Rahim wiped his palms on his khaki pants and carefully pulled on a pair of gloves. He looked more like a surgeon than a bushwhacker. "Let's get started."

I hoped I'd be paired with Imogen, but she ended up with Caleb, which I was not happy about, and I ended up with Mandy and Nick. At least I wasn't with Chad. He and Jason went off with Rahim. Our groups started out pretty close together, but as the afternoon went on we began to spread out.

None of us knew what we were doing. Mandy and Nick cut low-hanging branches, and I chopped at the underbrush with my hatchet, which wasn't really the right tool for the job. A power mower or Weedwhacker would have cleared the path in a fraction of the time. I had a feeling, though, that the path wasn't the point. They could have got a contractor in to do that. No, this was somehow supposed to be therapeutic.

I wasn't feeling it.

"So," Nick said at one point. "What's going on with you and Imogen?"

"Nothing," I said quickly. "We're friends."

"With benefits?"

I shook my head, my cheeks hot. "No. Anyway, even if we wanted to hook up, it's not like you ever get a minute of privacy here."

"What are you talking about?" Mandy said. "Imogen and *Alice*?"

"Yeah, why not?"

Mandy furrowed her forehead. "Well...uh, nothing."

I could practically see the thought written on her face. *But they're both girls!* I glared at her and whacked viciously at a shrub that was apparently made of Kevlar.

Eventually the conversation turned to the inevitable: Tara.

"What do you think really happened?" Mandy asked.

The blood on the log. The note. I hesitated, wondering if I should tell them. I couldn't imagine either Mandy or Nick having anything to do with Tara's disappearance. But Imogen and I had decided not to say anything to anyone yet...

I was opening my mouth to reply when a scream shattered the silence.

We froze for a second and then began to run through the brush in the direction of the sound. My heart was hammering, my breath shallow; thin branches whipped at my face as I ran.

I spotted Jason, Chad and Rahim first, also running—and then I saw Imogen. She was crouched on the ground, sobbing. Caleb was standing beside her, his machete dangling from his right hand.

"I hit her," he blurted out, letting go of the machete. "I—she just—"

"Oh my god, Imogen!" I dropped to my knees beside her. She was clutching her upper arm. Blood trickled from between her gloved fingers.

Nick knelt beside me. "Let me look," he said. "How bad is it?"

"I didn't mean to," Caleb said. "It was...she just...I..."

Jason picked up the machete from where it had fallen and took a few steps backward, away from him. "What the hell happened?"

Nick pulled Imogen's hand away from her arm. The gash was bad—three inches long and bleeding heavily. "She needs stitches," Nick said, looking at Rahim.

Rahim shook his head, clearly out of his depth.

"Right," Nick said. "I guess basic first aid will have to do. I've done the Red Cross courses." He pulled off his shirt, folded it a few times and pressed it tightly onto the wound. Imogen whimpered, and I rubbed her back in slow circles, not knowing what else to do. "Hold your arm up," Nick said. "That'll help slow the bleeding."

There was a crash behind me. "Oh shit," someone said.

Mandy had passed out. She was lying there with her half-unbuttoned shirt and bare midriff, white-faced and sweating amid the dead brown pine needles and green ferns.

Rahim squatted beside her, took off his safari vest and draped it over her. "Looks like she can't handle the sight of blood," he said. "It's a common autonomic response. Fainting, I mean. It's called vasovagal syncope—"

"Shut up," Chad said. "No one gives a shit."

I held Imogen's arm in the air and wondered if Rahim was going to pass out too. His face was ashen, and his lip was beaded with sweat.

"I'm so sorry," Caleb said. "Imogen? I am so, so sorry. Are you okay?"

She nodded but didn't look at him.

I turned on Rahim. "What the hell were you thinking?" I said furiously. "I mean, a goddamn machete? I told you not to give him a—"

"It was an accident," Caleb protested. "She stepped right in front of me just as I was lifting the stupid thing."

Blood was soaking through the shirt pressed against Imogen's arm, turning the light blue to a dark purple. I gripped it harder and thought again of the blood on the log.

And the note signed by Caleb.

I had to tell someone. Someone other than Imogen. But Warren was sick, and Claire was such a phony, and Rahim...well, maybe I could tell Rahim. But I wasn't sure he could actually do anything about any of this.

"Did I pass out?" Mandy asked, sounding like her usual self. She propped herself up on her elbows, avoiding looking toward Imogen. "Sorry. How embarrassing."

Rahim helped her into a sitting position. "Very normal," he said. "Very common. A lot of people have trouble with blood."

Mandy made a face. "Don't talk about it."

"Maybe we should *do* something?" I said. "Like, get Imogen back to the mess hall where we can take care of her?"

"Absolutely," Rahim said. "Can you stand up, Mandy?"

He held out a hand and helped Mandy to her feet. Chad was at Mandy's other side half a second later, swooping in to put an arm around her. "Here, lean on me," he said.

Imogen was the one who was injured and bleeding, but were they rushing to help her? Nope. It took a half-naked girl to provoke their chivalry, apparently.

"Hey." Jason leaned down, whispering into my ear so only Nick, Imogen and I could hear him. "I'm thinking that leaving all these machetes and hatchets and shit lying around isn't the best idea. So I'm gonna take them back and make sure they're locked the hell up. Okay?"

"Good idea. And keep *him* away from us." I pointed at Caleb, who was still standing there, his arms hanging uselessly at his sides.

"Can you guys manage…" Jason gestured at Imogen.

"Yeah," I said. "Nick's got first-aid training. And I can help. At least *I* won't pass out."

"Imogen, I'm going to wrap this around your arm…" Nick tied his now bloodstained shirt tightly. "Okay, put your hand here and squeeze. Can you walk?"

She nodded and stood up, pale and shaky.

"All right," Rahim said, clapping his hands as if he'd really been in control all along. "Let's get back to the mess hall and get everyone taken care of. Okay, troops?"

No one said anything. What was there to say?

There wasn't anything remotely okay about any of this.

SEVENTEEN

Caleb

According to Alice, I was some kind of machete-wielding, homicidal maniac. She wouldn't let me near Imogen when we got back to the mess hall and Rahim went to get the first-aid kit.

"Don't you think you've done enough damage?" she said when I offered to get Imogen some juice and a cookie. "She's not a toddler, you know. She needs medical attention, not cookies."

"She might be in shock," I said.

"She's not in shock," Alice said flatly. "If she was in shock, she'd be pale and clammy and breathing fast."

I ignored her and spoke to Imogen directly. "You want some juice?"

Imogen nodded, and I went into the kitchen and poured some juice into a chipped beige mug (*The meaning of life is to give life a meaning*). When I got back, Rahim had joined

Alice and Nick and was sitting beside Imogen, a big red first-aid kit open on the table beside him. I handed the juice to Imogen, but there wasn't much else I could do.

Chad had taken Mandy back to the girls' cabin to get a sweater or something. So much for Warren's gender segregation rules. They were probably hooking up while the rest of us watched Nick patch up Imogen's arm. Alice stroked Imogen's hair off her face, and it occurred to me that we were getting into some serious *Lord of the Flies* territory here. Was Tara our Piggy? The timing was off—Piggy dies after they've been on the island a while—but no doubt Alice would say I was Jack, the ultimate savage. And she would be Simon, of course, always standing on the moral high ground, making everyone else look bad. But this wasn't a novel. This was real. And one thing was for sure—the adults who were supposed to be helping us deal with our issues had some serious issues of their own. Warren and Claire had disappeared after lunch, and Rahim was clearly way out of his comfort zone.

"We all have our Wilderness First Aid certificates," Rahim said as he watched Nick unwind the shirt from Imogen's arm. "But I haven't had much opportunity to practice, so…"

"It's all right. I've got this," Nick said.

We all stood around and watched Imogen until she said, "You guys are freaking me out. Stop staring at me." The bleeding had stopped, but the cut looked like hell. Sticky with dried blood and probably already infected.

Who knew what nasty microbes had been lurking on the rusty machete blade.

"The cut doesn't look too deep," Rahim said. "Some antiseptic and a few butterfly bandages should do the trick." His hands shook as he fumbled through the first-aid kit, pulling out various packages to hand to Nick.

Nick swabbed the wound slowly and carefully, but Imogen flinched, and Alice said, "Let *me* do it. You're hurting her."

Imogen gave her a wan smile, but Nick continued to swab. "Almost done, Imogen," he said. "Rahim, could you hand me the butterfly bandages?" He bandaged the injured arm neatly, patted Imogen's shoulder and then went to wash his hands at the kitchen sink.

Rahim packed up the first-aid kit. "I'm going to check on Claire and Warren. You'll stay here with the girls?" he said to Nick and me.

We nodded, although I wasn't sure they wanted us there. Sure enough, as soon as Rahim left, Alice said, "You guys can go. We're good."

"You sure?" Nick said.

Imogen nodded. "I'm okay. Really. Alice will look after me." She shot me a look that clearly said, *Go away, you guys,*

Alice handed Nick his bloody shirt and said, "You should rinse this out before the blood sets."

"Thanks," Nick said, taking the shirt from her.

As Nick and I walked back to the cabin, I asked, "Have you ever read *Lord of the Flies*?"

He nodded. "Who hasn't? Isn't it, like, required reading in every eighth-grade class in the world? Civilization versus savagery, order versus chaos, blah, blah, blah. Why?"

"Ninth grade for me," I said. "But I've been thinking. We're on this island. And shit's gettin' real. Remind you of anything?"

"Well, I'm not signing up to be Piggy," he said. "I've been bullied enough for two lifetimes. We gotta take control. Do something bold before anything else happens."

"My thoughts exactly," I said. "We've got a fire to build tonight. Maybe someone will see the smoke and come and check it out."

"At the very least we can make some s'mores," Nick said.

"Like there're any marshmallows on this island…"

"At the very least," Nick amended, "I can burn this shirt."

*　*　*

Turned out that Nick knew what he was doing when it came to building a truly impressive bonfire. I belong to the *pile up a few logs, douse them with gasoline, and throw a match at it* school of fire building. Nick was more methodical.

"Textbook Boy Scout, with the badges to prove it," he told me. "My parents thought Cubs and Scouts would develop my macho side. They had no idea that a) I don't have a macho side and b) I only went because I had a huge crush on Toby Emerson, who lived next door and did all the things my dad wanted me to do. Baseball, long-distance loogie hocking, obsessing about cars. Toby dropped out of Scouts when he discovered alcohol and girls, but I stuck with it. I liked how organized everything was. So now I can tie a mean clove hitch, and I've got mad semaphore skills. Maybe if the fire doesn't work, I can make some flags. Or I can tie you up. Whatever you prefer."

"Not my thing," I said. "But it might come in handy if Chad needs some disciplining."

Nick laughed and picked up the lighter he'd swiped from the kitchen. He flicked it open and held it to some crumpled paper, and the flames licked the tepee of dry sticks he had placed on top of the paper. As the sticks burst into flame, Nick gently added small branches, one at a time. When he was satisfied that the fire was well and truly established, he let me add some driftwood. Not too much, and not all at once.

"Nice job," I said as I watched the flames shoot up into the night sky. "No one's going to think that's a camper's fire. You could burn someone at the stake on that thing."

"How very medieval of you," Nick said. "Did you have anyone in mind?"

I laughed. "If my stepdad was here I might be tempted, but contrary to what Alice would have you believe, I'm actually a pretty chill guy. Takes a lot to piss me off. A lot. Nobody here has even come close."

"Good to know," Nick said.

There was a brief, awkward silence. "That thing today…"
I shook my head. "Imogen stepped right in front of me.

It was totally an accident, but it shouldn't have happened. I mean, I should have been more careful. Not been so close to her. But…" I tried to push back the wave of guilt. "I was distracted, you know? Thinking about everything that's happened."

"Yeah. There's something off about this place, don't you think?"

I tried to make light of it. "Apart from, you know, one missing girl, three scarily inept adults and an incident involving a machete?"

"I'm serious," Nick said, meeting my eyes.

"Maybe." I nodded reluctantly. "To be honest, I've felt like that since we arrived. The sooner we get out of here, the better. I'll get some more wood."

Nick and I stayed up half the night, stoking the fire and dozing. The moon rose, a clear white semicircle. It hung low in the sky for a while and then disappeared behind thick cloud. The temperature dropped. No boats came to our rescue. No helicopters circled overhead, their spotlights sweeping the island. We gave up on our vigil around three in the morning and went back to the cabin after raiding the mess hall for granola bars. Nothing was locked up. The camp was utterly silent. No lights anywhere. No one had come looking for us. It was eerie. At the very least I'd thought Jason would miss us.

"Semaphore tomorrow," Nick whispered as we crawled into our beds.

"Roger that," I said.

WEDNESDAY

EIGHTEEN
Caleb

The gong woke me up. One. Two. Three. Four. Five. I'd been dreaming about my mom. Barry was hitting her, and she was wailing. *No, no, no, no, no.* What did five gongs mean again? I sat up and rubbed my eyes. No one else was awake. My Darth Vader clock said 5:00 AM.

Emergency meeting. That's what five gongs meant.

After a minute Nick moaned, hoisted himself out of bed and pulled his jeans on. "This can't be good," he said as he walked over to Jason's bunk and prodded him with his foot. "Rise and shine," he said. "Emergency meeting." Jason groaned and rolled away from him, muttering something about five more minutes. We didn't bother with Chad. The less we saw of him, the better.

I grabbed a hoodie and slipped my feet into my runners. Nick and I walked in silence to the mess hall. Just as we arrived, Jason ran up behind us, and we went in together.

The girls were already there, sitting together at one of the tables. They looked puffy-eyed and exhausted. Rahim looked even worse. His clothes were rumpled, his face gray and lined, his hair uncombed. He'd aged ten years overnight.

"What's going on?" I asked. "Where are Claire and Warren? Did someone find Tara?"

Rahim shook his head very slowly. "Sit down, boys. I'm afraid I have some very upsetting news."

Mandy shrieked and leaped to her feet. "I knew it. She was murdered, wasn't she? By someone on this island. By one of us." She looked around the room, her eyes wild. "Or by someone else who is here, hiding in the woods. A killer. We need to get OFF! NOW! Before he kills again."

Chad stumbled in through the door, looking half asleep. "I'm starving." He looked around the room. "What's going on?"

Everyone ignored him. "That's *enough*, Mandy," Rahim said, with more force than I would have expected of him. "We haven't found Tara. But something has happened to Warren." He blew out a long shaky breath before he spoke again.

This was going to be bad. Very, very bad. I could feel it in my gut.

"Warren…uh…" Rahim cleared his throat. "Warren is dead."

"Dead!" Mandy cried. "What do you mean? He can't be dead."

"What do you think he means?" Chad said. "Dude is dead."

"Not helping, *dude*," I said.

Rahim continued. "We don't know what killed him. At first we thought it was food poisoning, as you know, but it got worse and worse as the day went on. We did everything we could, but Warren passed away a few hours ago. As you can imagine, Claire is in shock. She's handed the reins over to me. I know this is frightening—first Tara and now Warren—but we have to work together to get through this. I'm here to help you—"

"If you say *process*, I am going to lose my shit," Alice broke in. "Seriously. No offense, Rahim, but I'm not talking to you about my feelings. Not now. Not ever. You can't help us."

She crossed her arms over her chest and glowered at Rahim. I felt a bit sorry for him, but she was right—he wasn't going to help us. If we wanted to get off this island, we'd have to figure it out ourselves.

"I'm going to take the kayak and get help," Jason said. "No way I'm waiting until Saturday to get out of here." He took off, heading out the door and letting it slam shut behind him.

"So what are the rest of us supposed to do?" Mandy moaned. "Sit around and wait to be killed? There's no way this is a coincidence. There's a dead body on the island, maybe two. I need to get out of here." She stood up and started to pace, her hands fluttering at her sides. "I need my meds," she said. "I can't breathe." She collapsed into a chair and hunched over, her shoulders rising and falling as she gasped for air. "Omigod, I'm gonna puke," she whimpered.

"She's having a panic attack. I used to get them sometimes," Imogen said. "Someone get a bowl." Alice ran to the kitchen and came back with a stainless-steel mixing bowl just in time for Mandy to retch into it. "It's okay, Mandy," Imogen said, rubbing Mandy's back. "It'll pass. Alice and I will sit with you. Jason's going to go for help. Caleb and Nick will make you some tea and toast." Her voice was calm and soothing. "You'll feel better soon, I promise." She looked up at Rahim. "Did she bring meds with her?"

Rahim nodded. "They're locked up. For emergencies."

"So get them," Imogen said. "This is an emergency. Do your job, for Christ's sake."

Rahim nodded again and shuffled out of the room.

"She's not wrong, you know," I said to Nick as we made tea and toast in the kitchen. I was glad to have something to do, something comforting and familiar, however insignificant. Bread in toaster, kettle on, tea in the pot, milk and sugar, butter and jam. Mandy may have been the only one having a panic attack, but we were all freaked out. We just showed it differently. "It's too much of a coincidence. First Tara, now Warren. It has to be connected. But how?"

"And why?" Nick said. "Tara was just a sad kid, and Warren was a buffoon. Who here would want to kill them?"

"I would have chosen Chad as my first victim," I said, and Nick flinched. "Too soon?" I asked.

He nodded and picked up the teapot, but before we could pour the tea, Jason came charging into the kitchen, looking grim.

"What's wrong?" I asked.

"I told the girls I'd come back for some supplies—didn't want to add to the panic—but I'm not going anywhere. Someone sabotaged the kayak. Huge hole in the hull. Looks like it was made by a knife. I dunno, man. This is getting desperate."

"No shit," Nick said. "I don't think tea and toast are gonna cut it when Mandy hears this."

"Rahim's getting her meds," I reminded them. "Probably Valium or Xanax or something. Maybe we should wait until she's calmer to tell her."

Jason nodded.

And then we heard Mandy screaming—a shrill, desperate scream. I dashed out of the kitchen, Jason and Nick on my heels.

Mandy was clinging to Rahim like he was the only thing that could save her from drowning. "Where are they?" she wailed. "Where are they? Did you take them?"

"What's she talking about?" I demanded.

"Mandy. Mandy, stop it!" Rahim tried unsuccessfully to pull away. "The drug cabinet has been broken into," he said over her shoulder. "All the meds are missing."

"What kind of meds?" I asked. "Anything Chad might like?"

"Don't be such a dick, Caleb," Imogen said.

"What? Like we weren't all thinking it," I said. "Am I right?"

"Harsh," Chad said. "I don't even do pharmaceuticals. Anyway, Imogen's the junkie. She's the one who'll try anything."

Rahim shook his head. "I think we need to focus on supporting each other right now. Accusing each other gets us nowhere."

Alice ignored him and turned on Chad. "You're the only one who's enough of a dick to steal people's medication from a locked cabinet."

"Locked cabinet?" He gave a nonchalant shrug. "Don't forget Jason, our resident safecracker."

Jason whirled to face him. "And when exactly would I have had the chance?" he demanded. "The only time I've been alone was just now, when I went to check out the kayak. And I agree with Rahim—this isn't getting us anywhere."

He was right. I put my hand on Mandy's shoulder, Rahim managed to extricate himself from her grip, and she collapsed against me. I patted her back awkwardly, and she went limp in my arms and started sobbing uncontrollably. "Can you get Mandy back to the cabin?" I asked Alice and Imogen. "Take the tea and toast with you. Maybe you can calm her down."

Alice looked mutinous, and for a moment I thought she was going to challenge me, but when Imogen took Mandy by the arm and said, "Come on, sweetie," Alice followed them out of the building. Chad wandered out behind them, whistling softly. Probably going to smoke some weed.

"Jason needs some help with the kayak," I told Nick. "We'll be back soon."

Nick nodded. "I'll be fine."

Rahim cleared his throat again. "My insulin was taken too." He sounded almost apologetic.

I'd forgotten that he was diabetic.

Nick looked worried. "Are you hyperglycemic?" he asked. "I mean, right now? Was your kit taken as well? When was your last shot?"

"My test kit's on my bedside table," Rahim said. "I haven't had a shot since last night. Normally, I'd have one in the morning, before breakfast."

"We should check your levels," Nick said. "My cousin Kelsey—my aunt's kid—has diabetes. She was diagnosed last year. I stay at their place when my parents get too unbearable, which means I practically live there. Kelsey's only eight...I've watched my aunt check her blood-sugar levels a million times."

Rahim nodded. "I'll check my levels. But I already know that I'll need insulin soon."

I had no idea how long a diabetic could go without insulin, but Rahim looked terrified. "We're on it," I said. "Be right back."

As Jason and I headed toward the staff cabin, I realized that Claire was probably inside with Warren's dead body. The only dead person I'd ever seen was my grandma. Open-casket funerals suck, especially when you're six years old and everyone wants you to say one last goodbye to a corpse. I'd taken one look at her and thrown up all over my new suit.

Now I knocked on the door and waited for Claire to open it. When she did, she looked like hell—chalk-white face, smudgy dark shadows under her eyes.

"We're sorry to bother you," I stammered. "Rahim needs his test kit. He's due for a shot, and he's got no insulin."

"What?" She put her hands to her face, pressing them against her cheeks like she was making sure she was still there or something. "He's got no insulin? Why?"

"The drug locker got broken into last night. Mandy's meds were taken, and Rahim's insulin is gone too."

Claire sighed and dropped her hands. A single tear rolled down her cheek. "I've been with Warren all night in our room. I didn't hear anything. I'm afraid I'm not going to be much use to you. Warren's death…" She leaned against the doorjamb, looking like she might faint. I stepped forward and helped her back into the cabin, easing her down onto one of the kitchen chairs. The doors to both the bedrooms were closed. I had no idea which one was Rahim's. The last thing I wanted was to walk in on a dead guy.

"Can you sit with me for a minute?" Claire asked, patting the chair next to her. Jason stayed standing in the doorway, his eyes moving around the room. Casing the joint.

"Uh, sure. I guess." I sat down and tried to think of something to say. All I could come up with was "I'm really sorry about Warren. He seemed like a good guy."

She sniffed, looking down at her lap. "Thank you for that, Caleb. He was a fine man. We were very happy together." Her voice caught a bit. "I need to ask you a favor. You and Jason."

"Sure," I said. "What is it?"

"This is going to sound…Never mind."

"It's okay," I said. "What is it?"

Claire shook her head and started to cry. "I can't."

"Can't what?" I glanced at Jason. He gave me a bug-eyed look and gestured helplessly. I turned back to Claire, who was sobbing now, hands over her face, shoulders shaking. "Claire, if there's anything we can do…"

"It's just…it's only Wednesday…and we're trapped here." Her words came out between gasps. "And Warren's dead."

"Jason and I are going to fix the…" I trailed off, realizing she didn't even know about the sabotaged kayak yet. "We'll do whatever we can to help you," I finished.

"Warren's…he's in my bed," she whispered. "I can't stay here with…a dead body. And by Saturday, he might… Won't he…"

Rot, I thought. Decompose. "Look, don't think about that now," I said quickly. How fast did a body start to decay, anyway? It was pretty warm in here. Would he start to smell? Or…worse? "We'll figure something out," I said. "Maybe we can move him to, uh…"

"The freezer?" Jason said.

"No," Claire said. "It's not big enough, and anyway…it seems wrong, you know?"

I nodded. "I know. Whatever we do, we'll…uh, treat him with dignity. Don't worry about that. Maybe we could put him in the kayak and send him out to sea?"

She shook her head. "I want to take him back to the mainland to be buried properly." She wrapped her arms around herself, hugging herself tightly.

I didn't like Claire all that much, but right now I felt awfully sorry for her. I half wanted to give her a hug, but I thought that might be inappropriate. I touched her arm lightly instead. "Of course. I mean, that makes sense."

Claire grabbed my hand and gripped it hard. "I need you to bury him."

Whoa. I had not seen *that* coming. "Uh, here? On the island?"

"You want us to dig a grave?" Jason said.

This was totally surreal. Like something out of a horror movie.

"Yes." She squeezed my hand. "I know it's a lot to ask, but I don't know what else to do. I can't stand the thought of him just lying somewhere. In a shed or…anywhere. I'll wrap him up in blankets so you won't have to look at him. I don't want to add to your trauma."

I didn't respond. I couldn't think of anything to say.

"When the boat comes on Saturday, I'll get Del to dig him up and take him home for a proper funeral." Her lower lip trembled, and she repeated, "I don't know what else to do."

I pulled my hand away from hers. "I need to get Rahim's test kit first," I said. Though really, what was the point in testing his blood sugar if there was no insulin to treat it?

"I'll get it for you," she said. "And then...tonight? Will you...?"

I looked at Jason. He shrugged. I didn't know what to say. I mean, obviously Claire wouldn't want to sleep in the same bed as a dead body. I got that. But burying him? I didn't even know if that was legal.

"You'll need to find somewhere in the forest where there's enough soil," Claire said. "There are shovels in the shed. And a wheelbarrow, I think. For the body. I'll talk to everyone and suggest a group campfire session after dinner, and you two can sneak away." She wiped her hand across her eyes. "I think it's best if no one else knows, don't you? It's so upsetting to think about."

"Can't we just cover him with a tarp and some branches?" Jason asked. "Burying him seems...I dunno—extreme. It's only for a couple of days. And it's not like there are bears or wolves on the island."

Claire shuddered. "I couldn't bear for the crows to get him. Please, guys, I need you to do this. For me..."

I nodded dumbly. Because what do you say to a hot young widow who asks you to dig a shallow grave for her husband's body?

NINETEEN
Alice

It was kind of crazy—maybe even *literally* crazy, under these circumstances—but I couldn't stop thinking about Imogen. Specifically, about kissing Imogen. Whether it was going to happen. What it would be like. The thing was, though I'd told Nick I was bi or pan—and I was pretty sure I was—I'd never actually kissed a girl. There was only one out lesbian at my school. Her name was Kelly, and she wore ultra-political T-shirts and was intimidatingly confident. I'd never even spoken to Kelly, let alone ventured into any of the Rainbow Club meetings that she organized.

So when it came to kissing girls, there hadn't been much in the way of opportunity.

We were sitting around the campfire, sparks shooting into the dark sky. Nick had told me earlier that he and Caleb had built a fire on the beach the night before, hoping someone would see the smoke and rescue us, but that seemed dumb to me now—it was obvious from the look of this fire pit that INTRO had fires on the island regularly. Even if someone did see smoke, I couldn't see why they would care.

There were eleven rough-cut log seats around the fire, but we were down to seven people. Tara was missing, Warren was dead, and Nick was back at the staff cabin, looking after Rahim, who was probably about to slip into a diabetic coma. People were dropping like flies all around us, but Imogen's thigh was pressed against mine and it was kind of exciting to think about what might happen.

I slipped my hand into Imogen's and she squeezed it tightly, and my heart did a little flutter.

God, since when was I so shallow?

Though apparently I wasn't the only one. Across the circle, I could see Chad making the moves on Mandy, sliding an arm around her waist. Caleb was staring into space like he was seeing something that no one else could see, and beside him Jason hunched forward, scuffing one heel aimlessly at the ground. I studied Caleb's expression for a minute, wondering if he was thinking about Tara. Wondering about that note I'd found. Wondering if he had anything to do with her disappearance.

We needed to confront him, I decided. Especially now that Warren was dead too. Someone had to get to the bottom of all this.

Claire was sitting alone, empty log seats on either side of her where Rahim and Warren should have been. "Uh, so, I thought each of us could share something," she said.

"A quote, perhaps, that you find comforting or inspiring. A prayer or a meditation."

No one said anything, which I interpreted to mean *God, that's a horrible idea, but since your husband just died, we'll go along with it.*

"I'm, uh, really sorry about Warren," Imogen said. "I mean, it's awful. So awful."

Claire nodded and burst into tears. Mandy squirmed away from Chad and rushed over to Claire, then stopped a foot away and awkwardly patted her shoulder.

"Sorry," Claire said, sniffing and wiping her eyes. "I want to support you all, but I just…I just…I don't think I can be here right now." She got to her feet. "Maybe you could do a sharing circle. Whatever you want. Would you mind if I…?" She gestured in the direction of her cabin.

"We'll be fine," Imogen said. "You should do whatever you need to do."

"Thank you," Claire said. "You're good kids. I…well, I appreciate it." She backed away from our circle, and I could see the tears on her cheeks in the light of the flames. Then she turned and ran down the trail, her slight figure disappearing around a bend.

"And then there were six," Chad said, tossing a stick onto the fire.

I shivered.

"Cold?" Imogen asked me. "Want to share this?"

She'd brought the gray INTRO blanket from her bunk and was spreading it across both of our laps. Under the blanket, she let one hand rest lightly on my thigh. I pretended not to notice.

"Thanks." I shifted closer. "This is nice. I mean, not this whole island thing. Obviously. But…"

"Yeah." Her fingers traced a pattern on my skin. "*This.*"

I slid my hand over hers. Our faces were only inches apart, but no way was I going to kiss her with the others sitting right there. "How's your arm?"

"Achy, but okay."

"That should never have happened. Seriously, could you imagine three more incompetent counselors?" I lowered my voice, even though Caleb was a good twenty feet away, on the other side of the fire. "I mean, machetes? I mean, seriously?"

Imogen laughed. "Alice, it was so totally my fault. I tripped and stumbled right in front of him."

"Still," I said.

"Seriously," she said. "If you'd seen it…I practically walked into the blade. I'm a total klutz. If anyone shouldn't be given a machete, it's me."

"Hmm. Has he even apologized?"

"Only, like, a hundred times."

"I don't trust him," I said. Imogen's hand on my thigh was a major distraction, but I pushed on, leaning close and whispering, "The note I found in Tara's bed? You have to admit, it's totally suspicious."

"Leaving her a note doesn't mean he killed her," Imogen whispered, her lips brushing against my ear. "Maybe he helped her escape somehow. Or maybe they met and chatted for a bit, and then he went to bed and she took off in the kayak. You don't know."

"Yeah, but…if he wasn't hiding something, why wouldn't he bring it up?"

"That's the suspicious part." She shook her head. "I don't know."

I glanced across the circle to look at Caleb, but he was gone. So was Jason. "Hey, Imogen. The guys…"

She pointed into the woods. "They snuck off a few minutes ago, right after Claire left. See?"

I squinted into the darkness and could see the bright point of a flashlight moving through the trees. I'd probably have seen them leave too if it wasn't for Imogen's hand on my thigh. "I wonder what they're doing," I said.

"Smoking a doob," Imogen suggested. "Anyway, who cares? I'm more interested in what we're doing."

I fidgeted nervously, tugging at a stray thread in the cuff of my hoodie. I wasn't sure what we were doing.

"Hey." Imogen touched my face. "Alice. I really like you, you know."

"Uh, I like you too." When Imogen said she liked me, it sounded sexy as hell. When I said the same thing, I sounded like a third-grader.

She leaned in, lips slightly parted.

"Wait, wait." I pulled back. "What about Chad and…"

Chad and Mandy were horizontal in the dirt on the other side of the fire.

"Relax," Imogen said, laughing. "They're busy."

Our eyes met. "Okay," I said. "Okay." I reached out, ran my fingers along the curve of her cheek and touched the silver ring that pierced her lower lip. Then I leaned in and kissed her, and she was kissing me back.

I'd kissed guys before, but this was different. This was *fierce*.

I slid my hand under her shirt, across the smooth warmth of her lower back, under the loose waistband of her cargo shorts to feel the soft curve of her hip.

A low wolf whistle interrupted us, and we flew apart. *Goddamn Chad.*

"You girls want to join us over here?" he called out.

I could barely see him—just a shape in the darkness—but Imogen and I were close to the campfire, so I guessed he could see us clearly enough.

"Piss off," Imogen said.

"Your loss!"

I snorted. "Asshole."

"Yeah." She looked back at me. "Where were we?"

But the mood was wrecked, and besides, Chad was probably watching now, and I wasn't going to make out with Imogen for his entertainment. "Let's get out of here."

"Back to the cabin?" She lifted an eyebrow, teasing.

"No." I shook my head. Imogen might have had plenty of other girlfriends, but I hadn't, and I wasn't sure I was quite ready for…well, for whatever might happen if we went back to the cabin. "Let's go see what Jason and Caleb are up to in the woods."

She groaned. "Seriously?"

"Don't you think it's suspicious? I mean, Claire left, so they could've smoked up right here. Or gone back to the guys' cabin if they wanted to be alone. Why head off into the woods?" I stood up.

"Fine," Imogen said. She sounded grumpy, but she got to her feet, leaving the blanket in a heap on the ground. "Fine, Detective Inspector Alice—what *is* your last name anyway?"

"Top secret," I said. "It'll cost you another kiss." I shoved my hands in my hoodie pockets. I couldn't believe I'd just said that.

"Deal," Imogen said.

We headed into the trees together, walking in the direction of the flashlight we'd seen. The woods around us got darker and darker as we went, and the light of the campfire behind us slowly faded into the blackness. If it wasn't for the half-moon, we wouldn't have been able to see anything at all.

"We're going to get lost," Imogen said after a minute.

"No we're not. We're still on that trail we made." A low-hanging branch scratched my cheek. "Ow. Well, sort of *half* made."

"Great. Scene of the machete incident. We're probably standing in a pool of my blood."

I shuddered, thinking of the blood on the log. Tara's blood. "Imo—"

"Shh." She grabbed my arm with one hand and whispered, "I think I heard something."

I looked in the direction she was pointing. "I don't hear anything…oh. Yeah, you're right. Come on. But let's be really quiet. I want to see what they're up to."

We walked as slowly and carefully as we could. It was hard to be silent, because we had to push branches aside and sticks kept breaking under our feet, but as we got closer, I stopped worrying. They weren't going to hear us, because they were making a ton of noise.

"What the hell?" Imogen whispered.

I shook my head, and we moved closer, listening. No voices. Just a rhythmic *scrape, thump, scrape, thump.*

Then the noise stopped, and I heard Caleb's voice. "You think that's deep enough?"

"Probably not, but it'll have to do," Jason said. "I'm wrecked. I'm dying here." He paused. "Sorry, man. Bad choice of words."

The flashlight turned on suddenly, and a pool of light spilled across the ground.

"Holy *crap*," Imogen whispered.

I just stared.

Jason and Caleb were standing over what looked like a newly dug grave.

"Ready?" Caleb said.

"As I'll ever be."

They bent down, and when they straightened up again, they were each holding one end of something long and, judging from their grunts, heavy. Something that looked an awful lot like a sleeping bag with a body in it. I felt like there was a boa constrictor tightening around my chest—I could hardly breathe.

"Tara," Imogen hissed. "They killed Tara." She turned to me, her voice barely audible. "Let's get out of here before they see us."

I tried to think rationally. "Shouldn't we…uh, confront them? Find out what's going on?"

Imogen gawked at me, eyes round as an owl's. "Are you out of your mind?"

"Yeah. I mean, no. You're right." I might have a black belt in karate, but I wasn't about to take on two guys who were twice my size. I turned to leave—and stepped on what must've been the thickest, driest stick in the entire forest. It snapped with a *CRACK*, a gunshot in the cool night air.

There was a loud thud—the guys dropping the body, I guessed—and then the flashlight beam swung toward us. We froze for a second, deer in the headlights, and Imogen let out a low whimper.

"Run!" I yelled. "Imogen, RUN!"

"Wait," Caleb shouted, starting to move toward us, a shovel in one hand. "It's not what it looks like."

I wasn't planning to stick around to hear his explanation, but Imogen was standing there, still as a statue, her face white in the stark light. "They killed Tara," she said again. "They killed Tara."

I grabbed her arm. "Come on. If they killed Tara, what do you think they're going to do to us?"

"It's not Tara," Jason said. "It's Warren."

I turned and stared at them both. "What?"

"Claire asked us to bury him," Caleb said. He sounded exhausted. "She was worried that he'd...uh, decompose."

Imogen sank to her knees in the dirt. "I'm going to be sick."

"Claire asked you to bury him," I repeated. My mind was struggling to keep up with its own thoughts. Not killers disposing of evidence. Just a nice little counselor-approved funeral in the woods. "That's unbelievably messed up."

"Yeah, well..." Caleb stopped a few feet away from me, like he was scared I'd run if he got too close. "She's not exactly firing on all cylinders right now. We had to sneak the body out of her bedroom in the staff cabin while Nick was in the other room with Rahim."

"This is crazy," I said. "Crazy. *She's* crazy."

"Off her nut," Jason agreed.

"Well, her husband just dropped dead. And she's trapped on this island with a bunch of teenagers she's responsible for..." Caleb trailed off.

"Yeah," I said. "She's really being *responsible*, asking you guys to bury a dead body." Imogen made a funny choking noise, and I put my hand on her shoulder and blew out a long, slow breath. "Imogen? You okay?"

She nodded. "I will be. Just..." She looked at Caleb. "Just give me a minute. I thought we were about to be killed. Seriously. We thought you guys had killed Tara and were burying her body."

Jason pulled back the top of the sleeping bag and shone the flashlight beam on what was unmistakably Warren's face. His very dead face. "See? Not Tara."

Imogen whimpered again and covered her eyes.

"Since you're here, you might as well lend a hand," Caleb said. "Burying a body isn't as easy as you might think."

TWENTY
Alice

The grave they'd dug was barely deep enough to fit the body, but the ground out here was hard and full of roots, and Jason's and Caleb's hands were a mess of blisters. Imogen and I shoveled the loose dirt on top of the sleeping bag until it was hidden.

"Aren't graves supposed to be, like, six feet deep?" I asked.

Caleb shrugged. "It's only until Saturday. Then we'll have to dig him back up so Claire can take his body home for a proper funeral."

"If no animals have a go at him first," Jason said.

"There are animals?" I looked around. "Like what? Bears?"

Caleb looked at me pityingly. "You're such a city kid. There're no bears here, Alice. But there are plenty of scavengers. Rats, for one. And mice."

"Mice eat people?" Imogen looked ill.

"Mice eat whatever they can find," Caleb said.

"Racoons too," Jason said. "And eagles."

We studied the thin layer of dirt covering what used to be Warren. "Maybe we should put some sticks or rocks or something on top," I said. "To protect him, you know?"

"Bit late," Jason said grimly.

No one said anything, because there was pretty much nothing you could say to that. We all stood there staring at each other, and then Imogen's hand slipped into mine. "I think it's a good idea," she said. "And maybe—don't make fun of this, you guys—maybe we should say something. Like, because this is sort of a funeral, isn't it? And it feels really wrong just leaving him here. In the woods."

"Sure," Caleb said. "It's a good idea, Imogen. A really good idea." His voice was gentle—kind—and if I hadn't still suspected he knew something about Tara's disappearance, I would've liked him for it.

We picked up armfuls of dead branches and laid them, crisscrossed, on top of the burial mound.

"Um, who wants to go first?" Imogen said. "Should we each say something?"

I made a face. It was the last thing I felt like doing. But for Imogen…"I'll start," I said. I picked up a branch and added it to the mound. "So, thanks for trying to help us by running this camp. My mom always said you were a good guy, and she'll be really sad to hear about what happened." I got a lump in my throat at the thought of my mother and rushed on before I could start to cry. "And, uh, I know it wasn't because of anything I did to the food, but I'm really sorry you got sick. And, well, died."

"That's it?" Imogen said.

I nodded. "Sorry. Not good at this kind of thing."

"This burying-bodies-in-the-woods-at-night thing?" Jason gave a low laugh, but he sounded depressed. "No kidding."

"You want to go next?" Imogen asked, handing him a stick.

Jason laid it where Warren's feet would be. "Sorry, man. You were a decent guy, and you didn't deserve to die like this."

Caleb cleared his throat and placed a slender branch across the pile. "I don't know what you believed in, but I hope you're somewhere good now. I'm sorry we had to do this tonight. Claire's pretty broken up, but she's going to make sure you get a proper funeral back in the city. And, uh, thanks for believing me about my stepdad and trusting me to come here." His voice wobbled a bit on that last part.

Imogen gave his arm an awkward pat. Then she pushed a large rock toward the grave, positioning it like a headstone, and she knelt beside it. "I didn't know you well, Warren, but I know you were kind. On the Zodiac, when I was puking, you didn't single me out or embarrass me in front of the others, but you whispered to me to hang in there, and I could tell that under all the tough-guy stuff, you actually cared." She paused for a moment and glanced up at me. "We're here burying you tonight at Claire's request, and I want you to know that we'll take care of her until we get out of here. All of us, you and Tara included." She wiped her eyes and stood up. "There. That's it."

We walked back through the woods together in silence. As stupid as it might sound, I was feeling a strange bond with the three of them. Like we'd been through something that no one else would ever understand.

But it wasn't over yet. It was only Wednesday, and unless there was a miracle, we were all stuck here—trapped here— until the Zodiac came to pick us up on Saturday morning.

Don't let your guard down, I told myself. Don't trust anyone. Though I did trust Imogen. I couldn't help it. And I wanted to trust Caleb and Jason…but I wasn't sure I could. Not with that note Caleb had written still unexplained.

"Look," Imogen said, pointing through the trees ahead of us. "We made it. There's the campfire." She put her arm around my shoulders.

I squinted through the trees at the ring of empty log seats around the dying fire, and I shivered.

It wasn't over yet.

THURSDAY

TWENTY-ONE

Caleb

When I woke up the morning after burying Warren, I could hardly move. Apparently I did not have a future as a grave-digger, which was a relief. A short cold shower woke me up but did nothing to unkink the knots in my arms and shoulders or get rid of the dread that clung to me like skunk spray. I hadn't wanted to come to the island in the first place, but I could never have imagined how totally insane this week would turn out to be. Insane and, if I was being honest, terrifying.

I decided to check on Rahim and Nick, make sure Rahim had survived the night. My stomach lurched when I considered that we might have another body to bury. I left Jason sleeping—Chad was AWOL, but that was nothing new—and headed over to the staff cabin.

Nick answered the door. The circles under his bloodshot eyes were a deep purple, and his skin was blotchy. I wondered if he had slept at all.

"How's Rahim?" I asked, glancing at the open door of one of the bedrooms. A motionless body lay on the bed. For a moment I was afraid he might be dead, but then I saw a slight movement and heard a low moan.

"Not so good," Nick said. "He started vomiting early this morning. I'm trying to get him to drink, but he's getting dehydrated. He needs IV fluids. And insulin, obviously. We have to get him some help. Soon. Otherwise…"

"I know," I said. "I'll stay with him so you can have a break. Is Claire sleeping?" The door to the other bedroom was closed. I understood why she'd bailed on us the night before, but I guess I'd hoped she'd be of some help today. Even if all she did was sit with Rahim. Or lead us in a sing-along.

"She went out when the sun came up," Nick said. "Said she was going to the woods to meditate or something. She's a total mess. I could hear her crying and talking to herself all night. Too bad Mandy's meds are missing. Claire could really use some."

"So could Mandy," I said. "Oh, Alice and Imogen are hooking up, I think. Also, Jason and I buried Warren in the woods last night. FYI."

Nick's eyebrows shot up. "You *what*?"

"Claire asked us to bury him. He was in her bed, and she was panicked about him, uh, decomposing."

"Jesus." He thought for a moment. "I've been here in the staff cabin the whole time. You guys were in Claire's room last night, fetching Warren's body? While I was in here with Rahim?"

"Yeah. I was surprised you didn't hear us, actually."

He shrugged. "I've been dozing on and off. Trying to stay awake, but…"

I nodded. "Alice and Imogen followed us into the woods and showed up in the middle of it all. They freaked out. Thought we had murdered Tara and were burying her body. We had to show them it was Warren. We ended up having this, uh, ceremony. Like a funeral, almost. It seemed wrong to just toss him in a hole, cover him up and walk away."

"That is all kinds of messed up," Nick said slowly. "Missing girls and impromptu funerals weren't on that glossy brochure my parents showed me." He smiled weakly. "Are you sure you don't mind staying with Rahim? I could use a shower, even a cold one, and some food."

I nodded. "We'll be fine. Take your time."

He stepped back into Rahim's room, leaned over him and said, "I'm going to grab a shower and get something to eat. Caleb's here. You won't be alone. I promise. You're gonna be okay." He reached out and patted Rahim's shoulder gently. When he walked past me on his way out, I thought I saw tears in his eyes. "I'll be back soon," he said. "Try and get him to drink something."

"I will," I said. "Don't worry."

Nick shut the door quietly, and I was left alone with Rahim. I looked around the cabin. There was a tiny kitchen area—just a bar fridge and a hot plate next to a small sink. A glass of water sat on the counter next to the sink, so I took it into the bedroom and helped Rahim sit up to drink it. He took two sips and then waved the glass away.

"No more," he whispered, and I helped him lie down again. His skin was pasty and mottled, and he was almost panting for breath. After a while he seemed to fall asleep. I hoped he hadn't slipped into a coma. I had no idea how to tell the difference, other than to try to wake him—and that seemed unkind. I felt for his pulse. His heart was racing.

I sat by the bed in a hard chair, watching Rahim breathe, but eventually I got restless and pulled out my sketchbook. It felt wrong to draw someone who was that out of it, so I went back into the main room and did a couple of sketches of what was on the table—a dirty coffee cup with lip gloss on the rim, a crumpled piece of paper towel and a small red plate with crumbs on it. But I couldn't even get the plate right. It looked like a melted Frisbee. I got up and wandered around the cabin, tried unsuccessfully to find a comfortable position on the lumpy brown couch and then stood up again and opened the door to Claire's room. I wasn't sure why. Boredom. Curiosity.

An unmade double bed took up most of the floor space, and the room smelled of vomit and lilacs, as if Claire had spritzed the room with perfume to mask the stench of Warren's death. A small bookcase next to the bed held a row of books, some binoculars, a few shells, a collection of bird skulls, a couple of feathers and an ugly pottery candlestick. I ran my fingers along the spines. *The Power of Now, Helping Teens Handle Tough Experiences, The Happiness Project, The Big Book of Icebreakers, Awaken the Giant Within, Reclaiming Youth at Risk.* Next to *Shouting at the Sky: Troubled Teens and the Promise of the Wild* was a bright-yellow book called *You Are a Badass: How to Stop Doubting Your Greatness and Start Living an Awesome Life.*

I felt kind of stalker-ish being in Claire's bedroom, but I needed to distract myself while I waited for Nick, so I pulled *You Are a Badass* from the shelf. I could see something in the gap between the books. Something that made me drop the book as if it were on fire. I could read about living an awesome life later.

Right now I had to figure out a way to pick up an empty prescription bottle without smudging whatever fingerprints were on it. Of course, Mandy's would be there...and at least one of the counselors'. Still, probably better not to add my own to the mix.

I grabbed a piece of Kleenex from a box on top of the shelf, picked up the empty pill bottle by its lid and read the label. *Mandy Ostrofer. Xanax (Alprazolam) 1 mg. 30 tabs.* I looked around for something to put it in. I found a ziplock bag in a drawer in the tiny kitchen. There was no way to know how many pills had been in the bottle when Mandy came to the island, and I had no evidence that the pills had been used for anything criminal, but it was still evidence. I just didn't know of what. Could Tara have broken into the locked cabinet and taken an overdose once she was out on the water? It seemed unlikely, but it was possible.

I sat on the couch until Nick came back, his hair still wet from the shower. When I showed him my discovery, he shrugged. "Maybe Claire took them. But if so, they didn't work—she was freaking out last night."

"But why hide the bottle?" I asked. "And how come all the pills are gone?"

"No idea. You don't think Claire would off herself, do you? Should we go look?"

Before I could answer, Rahim started to cough and then choke. Nick ran to his side and helped him sit up and vomit into a bucket by the bed. "Go look for Claire," he said, waving me away. "Rahim doesn't need both of us."

I nodded and left the cabin, making my way down to the beach, the pill container in my hoodie pocket. I needed to think, to sort things through in my mind before I told everybody else what I had found. If Claire had killed herself, five minutes wouldn't matter one way or the other.

I was about to climb down the path onto the beach when I saw Chad and Claire. They were sitting on a log together, and Chad had his arm around her shoulders. At least I wouldn't have to search the island for her body. As I watched, he pulled her closer to him and ran his hand up her thigh. She leaned into him, and his hand moved higher. Then she stiffened and pushed him away. I couldn't hear much of what she said, just the occasional word— *young, crazy, stop*—but whatever she said made Chad put his hands up in a gesture of surrender.

Claire stood up, moving away from him and scrambling up the embankment to the path. I slipped into the shadows, and she ran past me, toward the staff cabin. Chad lit a joint, inhaled and slid down so his back was against the log. Then he exhaled loudly and said, "Chicks!" before he closed his eyes and appeared to doze off. What a prince.

TWENTY-TWO
Caleb

I left the beach and found everyone else in the mess hall, more or less awake and finishing breakfast. After I ate some French toast (courtesy of Jason and Mandy), I filled them in on Rahim's condition and the scene on the beach.

"Chad was with *her*?" Mandy said. "She's, like, old." The look of befuddlement on her face would have been funny under other circumstances. Right now it was just really sad.

"She's everything Chad wants," Alice said. "Single and female."

Mandy looked confused. "But I'm single and female. And a lot hotter than she is. I don't get it."

Alice sighed. "Forget it. He's a jerk."

"And there's something else," I said, pulling the pill bottle in its plastic bag out of my pocket and holding it up. "I found this in Claire's room, behind some books."

That got Mandy's attention. She screeched, "Those are mine!" and lunged for the bottle.

I held it up where she couldn't reach it. "It's empty, Mandy. And it's evidence."

"Evidence of what?" Imogen said.

"Not sure," I said. "But it's definitely a clue."

"Caleb's right," Alice said. "It is evidence. My mom's always going on and on about the chain of evidence—who found it, where and when it was found, who secured it, who had access to it. If you mess up the chain of evidence, your case can get thrown out of court."

I was surprised to hear Alice, of all people, supporting me. I gave her a grateful nod. She started to grin back but quickly broke eye contact and looked away.

"So the chain of evidence is important even if you don't know what the crime is?" Imogen asked.

"Especially if you don't know," Alice replied. "Let's see what we have so far. Does anyone have any paper? And a pen?"

No one moved. I sighed. So much for hiding my sketching habit. I pulled out my notebook, ripped a piece of paper out and handed it to her along with my pen. She stared at the paper as if she had never seen anything like it before.

"One empty Xanax bottle," I said, putting it on the table. "Picked up with Kleenex and sealed in a plastic bag. Should be good for a few prints."

Alice nodded and started writing.

"Missing insulin," Jason said. "Missing radio part. Missing girl."

"Let's start with physical evidence," Alice said. "The things we actually have. We'll come back to the missing stuff later."

"Kayak with a hole in it," Imogen said. "Can't exactly put that in a bag for safekeeping. Maybe we could find some rope and cordon it off?"

"Good idea," Alice said. She hesitated and exchanged a long glance with Imogen, who was sitting beside her. Imogen nodded, and Alice let out a shaky sigh. "Okay. Uh, this may not be anything, but I saw blood on a log on the beach, near where the kayaks are kept. At least, I think it was blood. Plus, there was a footprint nearby." She looked right at me. "The footprint was pretty big, Caleb."

"So you think I killed Tara?" I tried to sound composed, but I could feel my heart speeding up. "Because of a footprint on the beach?"

"It crossed my mind," Alice said.

"I'm not a…I hit one person, Alice. One. A person who was hurting my mom. That's it." My voice was low and even, but I wanted to yell at her, tell her not to judge me, tell her what an idiot she was being. If I was a violent, out-of-control guy, I'd have punched her by now. Lucky for her, I wasn't.

"It rained when we were doing the boat ceremony," Alice said. "So that footprint had to have been left the night she disappeared. Late, after the rain stopped."

I thought back. Waking early, sketching on the beach…
it probably *was* my footprint. "I went to the beach that
morning," I said. "To be alone, not to kill anyone. I know
you think I'm just a big dumb brute with rage issues, but I
liked Tara. Why would I kill her?"

Alice and Imogen exchanged another long, meaningful
look. "You tell me," Alice said. "It's obvious you're hiding
something."

"I'm not. I'm really not." I shrugged. "Look, I don't know
what else I can say."

"I know you met her on the beach the night she disappeared." Alice slipped her hand into her pocket and pulled
out a piece of paper. She laid it down on the table in front of
me. There was a single sentence written on it:

*MEET ME ON THE BEACH TONIGHT AFTER THE OTHERS
ARE ASLEEP.*

—CALEB.

"What the…?" It was my name, but I'd never seen the
note before. And I sure as hell didn't give it to Tara. "I didn't
write that," I said.

"It's the right size for your notebook," Alice pointed out.

"My notebook is unlined. I use it for sketching. See?"
I shoved the notebook at her, but she wouldn't take it.
"You're in there. So is Tara. So is Nick. Have a look. As far
as I know, drawing isn't a crime."

I riffled through the notebook until I found a sketch of
Alice and Imogen holding hands on the beach. I held it up
in front of her. She flinched.

"It isn't even my handwriting," I said. "Look." I grabbed the pen from her and scrawled *meet me on the beach*. "See? Not even close."

Alice inspected my writing and said nothing.

"He's right, Alice," Imogen said. "We shouldn't jump to conclusions. Anyone could have written that note. What we don't know is why Tara decided to go."

"I know why," Alice said. "She went because she thought Caleb wrote it." She glanced up at me and met my eyes. "She liked you, Caleb." She looked around at the others. "She said he was cute and sweet. Tara was vulnerable, and someone took advantage of that. If it wasn't Caleb…"

"It wasn't."

"I couldn't really see it," Alice said, her words coming out in a rush. "I mean, I couldn't really imagine you hurting her. I thought maybe you'd met her on the beach and then you guys had a fight and she took off. But I couldn't figure out why you'd hide that." She looked down at the note and then at my own scribbled words. "It really doesn't look anything like your writing. But Tara wouldn't have known that…"

"You said it yourself, Alice," Jason said. "We should look at the physical evidence. Caleb has explained the footprint on the beach. Add Tara's note to your list, and let's move on."

Alice scribbled for another minute and then said, "We need to list all the suspects now. Can we agree that it's not one of us?"

"Suits me," I said. Everyone laughed nervously.

"Maybe there's someone else on the island," Jason burst out. "Someone with a reason to want Tara dead. Or maybe Warren killed her and then killed himself."

I saw Mandy's eyes widen, and she started to pace the room, her hands flapping at her sides. "Oh my god, that's what I've said the whole time, and no one ever believes me!" She hurried back to the table and clutched Jason's arm. "You really think there could be someone else on the island? A serial killer? Someone who killed Tara and Warren?"

"Jason's got a rich fantasy life, Mandy. No one else is on the island," Imogen said.

"That scary guy from the boat," Mandy moaned. "The one who said he'd wear our bras and boxers. Maybe it's him."

I looked at her, startled. Del the Zodiac guy? Was that possible?

Imogen put her arm around Mandy. "Sit down with me and concentrate on your breathing. In through the nose, out through the mouth, like we practiced. You're not going to be alone. Nothing is going to happen to you. We're going to stay together, right, guys?"

"Right," I said. "All for one, and one for all. Except for Chad, of course."

Alice looked up from her list. "Could it be Chad?" she said. "Let's review the evidence." She cleared her throat. "The note."

"He could have written it," Jason said. "And he was out of the cabin the night Tara disappeared. Maybe he killed her and hid her body somewhere."

"Also, he had that fight with Warren," Imogen added. "Remember? Warren put Chad in a headlock, and Chad was pissed."

"Plus he's a jerk," I said. "Not that being a jerk is a crime. But I think we're ignoring one key piece of the puzzle."

"What's that?" Alice asked, her eyes narrowing behind her glasses.

"Chad's too dumb to plan any of this," I said. "He's annoying for sure, but I think he's pretty harmless, and he couldn't plan his way out of a paper bag. Too much weed. Not enough brain cells. And what's his motive? The dude's finest ambition is to get baked and get laid."

Jason nodded. "You're right. Chad's too freakin' thick. And I didn't kill her. I can't see any of us doing that. I vote for the Warren theory. He lures Tara to the beach for a snog, she tells him to take a hike, he bashes her on the head with a rock. Maybe he noticed she had the hots for our Caleb, so he signed the note that way. She freaked out when she saw who it really was, and—"

"Warren would never have looked at Tara," Alice said dismissively. "Mandy, maybe, but not Tara."

"Thanks, I think," Mandy said. "Warren was hot."

Alice rolled her eyes at Imogen, who patted Mandy's hand.

"Bottom line, our chain of evidence doesn't really lead us anywhere," Alice said, "and the missing stuff—Tara, the insulin, the radio part—well, that's all it is. Missing." She put down the list, took off her glasses and rubbed her eyes.

"And we still don't know how the Xanax bottle got into the bookshelf," I said. "I think we need to make a plan to keep everyone safe until the boat comes and we can call the cops."

"And an ambulance for Rahim," Imogen said. "Unless you think Rahim did this to himself."

"No way," I said. "He's kind of a goof, but he's a good guy."

No one disagreed, so I continued. "Nobody goes anywhere alone," I said. "And we'll all sleep in one cabin tonight. Even Chad. Agreed?"

Everyone nodded, although the girls didn't look very happy. Sharing a cabin with Chad was no one's idea of a good time but, like it or not, he was one of us.

When Imogen got up to clear the dishes, I said, "I'm going to get Nick. He needs to know what's going on. Claire can look after Rahim for a while. Let's meet back here in an hour."

"I'm coming with you, big guy," Jason said. "Nobody goes anywhere alone, remember? Even you."

As we left the hall, Alice scurried up after us. I resisted the urge to swat her away like a mosquito.

"Hey, Caleb," she said. "Can we talk a sec?"

"Sure." I kept walking.

"I was only trying to make sense of the evidence. The note, the footprint."

When I didn't reply, she said, "You judged me too. You know you did. Right from the start, making that crack about me being an alcoholic or an anorexic."

"Yeah, but I didn't accuse you of murder. Once I got to know you a bit, I gave you the benefit of the doubt. But I guess that's not your style."

We had reached the staff cabin, and I turned to face her. "I'm going to check on Nick and Rahim. Jason will walk you back to the girls' cabin. Also, you might consider saying 'I'm sorry' sometimes. I find it usually works really well. So, for the record, I'm sorry I jumped to conclusions about you."

She looked up at me. "I'm sorry too, okay? And I'm scared. Really scared."

TWENTY-THREE

Alice

I'd never felt less safe in my life—but it still bugged me that guys always acted like girls needed to be protected.

Caleb could have said, *Hey, Jason and Alice, how about you two walk back to the girls' cabin together?* Or *Hey, Jason, Alice will walk you back to the guys' cabin.* But no. He just announced that Jason would walk *me* back.

Because sexism.

"I have a black belt in karate, you know," I told Jason.

"Good," he said. "The way things are going, that might be useful."

"Yeah. Though look at Warren. I mean, he was about as tough as you can get, and now…"

"Dead and buried."

"Yeah." My mind was still circling back over the conversation, the theories, the evidence. Trying to make the pieces fit. Plenty of evidence pointed at Chad, but I had to admit that Caleb had made a really good point: Chad didn't have the brains to cover his tracks.

We were missing something, but what? We'd basically searched the whole island when we were looking for Tara...

"Jason," I said, stopping abruptly.

"What?"

"The staff cabin. That's where the Xanax bottle was. And it's the one place we haven't really searched properly."

"Kind of awkward, with Claire and Rahim there."

"Rahim's barely conscious," I said. "Look, go catch up with Caleb. You guys tell Claire that the girls need her."

"Why?"

"So you can search the cabin, obviously."

"No, I mean why would you guys need her?"

I threw up my hands. "Use your imagination. Tell her I found a bottle of stove alcohol in the shed and you're scared I'm going to drink it and go blind because I'm such a lush. Or that Imogen and I had a fight and now Imogen's threatening to kill herself—"

"Or that you are?"

"As if," I said. "Make it believable." Then it struck me. "Tell Claire that Mandy thinks she's pregnant, and she's freaking out."

Jason frowned. "And when she comes running to the rescue?"

"Then we try and keep her occupied with some drama while you and Caleb search the staff cabin."

"Okay." He hesitated. "You think Mandy will go along with it? Pretending she's pregnant?"

"I'll give her a heads-up," I said. "Go on."

"You'll be okay on your own?"

"Black belt, remember?"

Jason nodded and took off down the path.

I sprinted as fast as I could the rest of the way to the girls' cabin. Black belt or not, I didn't want to be out there alone any longer than necessary.

* * *

"Why do I have to be the pregnant one?" Mandy asked.

Imogen and I exchanged glances. If there was ever a time for tact… "You're the most heterosexual," I said, and Imogen stifled a giggle.

"Oh, okay." Mandy relaxed. "I thought maybe you were saying I looked fat or something."

I rolled my eyes. "Seriously? We're investigating a possible murder, Mandy. Maybe two. And even under normal circumstances, I wouldn't give a shit about your weight."

"Anyway," Imogen said, grinning, "curves are hot."

I glared at her—I'm basically the opposite of curvy—but moved on. "Mandy, you have to look like you're really upset, okay? Like you've been crying and you're all hysterical. Do that thing where you freak out and can't breathe—"

Imogen cut me off. "She means, if you can pretend you're having a panic attack, that'll keep Claire here with you. Try to buy the guys enough time to search the cabin."

"Okay. Should I say who the father is?"

"Doesn't matter," Imogen said. "Just keep her here."

"Think about not having any Xanax," I said. "Think about how you're trapped on this island, and people are dying, and we're all in danger—"

Imogen clapped her hand over my mouth. "Alice!"

"Just trying to get her in the mood," I said.

"I can act, you know," Mandy said stiffly. "I was Juliet in our school play a couple of years ago."

"Yeah, well, don't get all Shakespearean about it—" There was a knock at the door. "Who is it?" I called.

"It's Claire."

"Start crying," I whispered. "And remember—no boat, no Xanax, bodies piling up, etcetera." Then I raised my voice. "Come on in."

Claire opened the door and hurried over to Mandy, her forehead creased with concern. "Jason told me. I'm so sorry you're going through this, Mandy."

"There's been all this stuff going on." Mandy gave a hiccupping sob that sounded more or less genuine. "And my period's super late. I haven't even seen a *doctor*. I can't have a *baby*, Claire. I can't be a *mother*. I want to get an abortion."

Claire put her arm around Mandy's shoulders. "Whatever you decide to do, we'll make sure there's someone there to support you. Okay? It'll be all right. You'll get through this." She looked at Imogen and me. "How about you two give us a few minutes?"

"Sure," I said, heading for the door. "Take as much time as you need."

The longer the better.

*   *   *

Imogen and I sat with our backs against a tree, twenty feet or so from the cabin.

"Claire handled that well," Imogen said. She sounded surprised.

"It's her job." But I'd been surprised too: Claire hadn't handled anything well since Tara disappeared.

"Yeah, I guess. But you never know about that stuff. She could've turned out to be an anti-choice fanatic and started lecturing Mandy on her responsibilities. That would've sucked."

I gave her a gentle shove. "Mandy's not actually pregnant, remember? Well, not as far as we know."

"I know. Still, who wants to listen to that?"

"Yeah," I said. "Though, whatever, right? As long as they keep talking long enough for Jason and Caleb to get a good look around." Imogen nodded, but her forehead was furrowed, and she seemed distracted. "What is it?" I asked. "What are you thinking about?"

"Oh…just…when we do get out of here?" She hesitated. "Never mind. It's nothing."

I narrowed my eyes at her. "Tell me. What is it?"

"I was thinking I wouldn't mind doing that kind of job."

"What kind of job? What are you talking about?"

She met my eyes for a second, then looked away. "What Claire does. Counseling."

I was taken aback for a second—I wasn't filled with warm and fuzzy feelings about counselors at the moment—but then I thought about how Imogen had been with Mandy when she was freaking out for real. "Well, it's good to have goals, right?"

"I wouldn't know, really." She chewed on her lower lip. "I'm not sure I've ever really had any. My stepbrother, MBA guy—once he stopped devoting himself to pissing off our dad, he was all about setting goals. But I've just kind of…floated through stuff, I guess."

"After this week," I said, "like, if we actually get out of here…" I hesitated.

She looked at me.

"Um. Are you going to go back to getting high all the time?" I asked.

Imogen shrugged. "I don't know. Maybe. Probably not." She picked up a piece of bark that was lying on the ground and crumbled it between her fingers. "I didn't actually get high as much as everyone thought I did."

I'd kind of suspected that. "Well, I think you'd be good at counseling," I said. "You notice stuff about people."

"Yeah?"

"Yeah. I could totally see you as a counselor."

"Well, whatever," Imogen said. "At this point, my only goal is to stay alive."

Our eyes met. "Are you scared?" I whispered.

She nodded, and her brown eyes were shinier than they should be. "Terrified."

I swallowed hard. "Me too."

A few minutes later the cabin door opened, and Claire stepped out.

"Oh shit," I muttered under my breath. That hadn't been enough time—there was still no sign of the guys.

"It's okay," Imogen said. "We'll stall." She stood up. "Claire?"

Claire walked toward us. "I'm glad you sent for me," she said. "Mandy's feeling better, and we've scheduled a full session for tomorrow morning to talk over her options. And when we get back to the mainland, I'll make sure she's connected with some local resources."

"When we get back," Imogen repeated hollowly. "Aren't you scared, Claire?"

"Of what? Of going home?"

"No." Imogen shook her head. "I mean, what happened to Tara, and Warren…what if someone on the island is, I don't know, killing people."

"That's absurd." Claire brushed her hair away from her face. "Sad as it is, I'm sure Tara's disappearance was an attempted suicide—she could still be alive, you know. And Warren, though I'm devastated by his death, it must have been food poisoning, or a heart attack, or some other underlying medical condition."

I stared at her. Were the other campers and I caught up in some crazy conspiracy theory when all we had was a tragic coincidence? But then, what about the blood on the beach?

"As long as we're here, we're in limbo," Claire continued, her voice breaking slightly. "What I'm scared of is going home and realizing that Warren is really gone. Being in our apartment with all our things…the chair where he sits, and the books on his bedside table, and his dirty clothes in the laundry hamper…and realizing that he's never coming back."

"Oh…" Imogen reached out a hand toward Claire. "I'm so sorry."

Claire shook her head. "I can't let myself think about it now. We have to hang on. Only two more nights until the boat comes for us."

I heard a twig snap and squinted through the trees. Someone was coming down the trail.

"I'm going to head back and see how Rahim is doing," Claire said. "Nick has been an absolute godsend. He should go into nursing. Or medicine."

First Imogen and now Nick? It was like goddamn career week.

Jason and Caleb emerged into the clearing, nodded hello to Claire as she headed back toward her cabin, and joined me and Imogen.

"That was awfully close," I said.

"But awfully successful," Jason said. He looked over his shoulder to make sure Claire was gone, then ran back a short distance and grabbed something from behind a large bush. He held it up for us to see—a metal box of some kind, the size of a microwave oven. "Check it out."

"Come on," Caleb said. His voice was grim. "Let's go into your cabin and see what we have."

TWENTY-FOUR
Alice

The five of us—Nick was still with Rahim and no one knew where Chad was—sat on the floor around the object the guys had found under Warren and Claire's bed.

"It's a digital safe," Jason said. "The kind you get in fancy hotel rooms."

It looked pretty heavy-duty. "I don't suppose you found a key to go with that," I said.

Jason smirked. "You forget who you're talking to. Locks are my friends."

Imogen pushed a few random numbers. Nothing happened. "You know the code or something?" she asked.

Jason shook his head. "Given the quality of everything else around here, I'm guessing they cheaped out on the safe too." He gave it a gentle shake, like he was feeling the weight of it. "And if I'm right, I can bounce it."

"Bounce it?" Caleb asked.

"Yeah. See, the code slides open a dead bolt—well, two dead bolts usually." He gestured to the non-hinged side of the door. Then he lifted the front edge of the safe a few inches and dropped it against the floor, turning the locking knob at the same time. "If it's a decent safe, the dead bolts will have counterweights. Cheap safe? No counterweights, so you can bounce the dead bolts open for a sec." He dropped it again, turning the lock.

"It's not working," Mandy said.

"Give me a freakin' minute. It sometimes takes a few tries…" Jason dropped the front edge of the safe again, and again, and again… "And we're in," he said, swinging the door open. "Excellent."

"No way," Imogen said, and Jason grinned.

"My area of expertise," he said. "I can pick locks of all kinds. Not that I have any of my tools with me. Luckily, safe bouncing doesn't require anything but good timing."

We looked inside, practically knocking our heads together to see. "Here," I said. "Let me take the stuff out, okay? One thing at a time."

"Why you?" Caleb said. "Jason and I found the safe."

I ignored him. "And we should try to preserve any fingerprints. In case any of this ends up being evidence." I looked around. "I don't suppose anyone has a pair of gloves."

Mandy pulled a ziplock bag out of her pocket. "Would this work?"

I took it from her, shook out what appeared to be muffin crumbs and slipped it over my hand. There was a shelf across the middle of the safe. What looked like a bright-fuchsia purse—Claire's, presumably—was jammed into the bottom half, beneath the shelf, and an assortment of objects sat on top of it.

"Cell phone," I said. "Locked though." I looked at Jason, who shook his head.

"Not my thing," he said. "Sorry."

Mandy sighed. "I miss my phone so much..."

"Another cell, and another." I put them down on the floor, side by side.

"Claire, Rahim and Warren," Caleb said. "Gotta lock up your valuables if you're spending a week on an island with a bunch of delinquents."

I nodded, picking up a brown leather wallet and riffling through it—which wasn't easy with a plastic bag for a glove. "It's Rahim's. Forty bucks, driver's license, credit cards, library card...nothing interesting." I put it down beside the phones. "Any guess who this one belongs to?" I held up a camo-patterned wallet.

"Get on with it," Caleb said.

"Credit cards. Two hundred bucks. C-Tow membership. Driver's license..." I put it down. "And there's a necklace here that must be Claire's. That's it for the top shelf."

"I'm going to be so disappointed if we don't find anything," Imogen said. "Jason, are you sure you can't hack into the phones?"

He shook his head.

"There's still this," I said, pulling out the purse.

Mandy's eyes widened. "Oh my god."

I froze. "What? What?"

"That's an Ethan K bag! It's crocodile! Do you know what those cost?"

Imogen laughed. "Claire the vegan has a crocodile purse? That's awesome."

Mandy reached out to stroke it, but I pulled it away. "Fingerprints, Mandy!"

"Like, five thousand dollars, I bet," Mandy said. "Or more. Like, a lot more."

She was practically drooling. I didn't get it. Why would anyone spend that on a bag? I opened it. "Wallet," I said, pulling out a slim turquoise leather wallet. "Same as the others. Cards. Fifty bucks. Nothing personal." I opened the purse wider. There was a plastic bag stuffed in there. I pulled it out and opened it. "Holy shit." I tipped the contents onto the floor: Rahim's insulin bottles—empty, unfortunately— and a jumble of used syringes.

"No way," Imogen breathed. "Does that mean…what does that mean? Did Claire…?"

"Careful," Caleb said. "Don't want anyone getting jabbed."

I picked up the bottles one by one, lining them up on the floor, and began removing the syringes. In my neighborhood, you get plenty of practice picking up used needles. There are sharps containers mounted on the telephone poles for disposing of them.

"No way," a voice said from behind me. "You guys are shooting up?"

Chad was back.

"Not exactly," Caleb said. "Where've you been, anyway?"

"Took a nap." Chad dropped to his knees beside Jason. "Holy shit. Is that Rahim's insulin? Where'd you find this?"

"Under Warren and Claire's bed," Caleb said.

"Holy shit," Chad said again. "Hey, what's that?" He reached out to pick something up, but Jason grabbed his arm.

"Mind the needles—" Jason stopped abruptly as he spotted what Chad had seen among the syringes. "No way."

Caleb and I both reached for it, but I got there first. I picked it up, a twisted little piece of metal with a wire dangling from it.

"What is that?" Mandy asked.

"Missing piece from the radio," Jason said.

Mandy clasped her hands together like she was praying. "Can you fix it?"

"I said I was good with electronics, not that I could work miracles." Jason inspected it closely, his face nearly touching my hand. "It's been smashed up."

I put the radio piece down beside the row of bottles. "So that's it, isn't it?"

"What?" Jason said.

"This was in the counselors' cabin. Rahim didn't dump his own insulin, and Warren...well, he's dead and buried." I pointed in the direction of the woods.

"Buried?" Mandy's voice rose.

"Metaphorically speaking," Caleb said quickly, and I realized we hadn't filled Mandy in on our nighttime adventures. The spur-of-the-moment funeral popped into my mind; it felt completely surreal.

"Anyway," I went on, "that just leaves Claire, doesn't it? This stuff…" I nodded at the safe in front of me. "She hid this stuff."

"Not necessarily. Warren could have stolen the insulin and killed himself with it," Jason argued. "He could've injected himself and hidden the evidence before he got too sick."

"Why would he though?" I asked.

"Because he killed Tara," Caleb said. "Maybe it was an accident, and he got rid of the body to cover it up, but then he was overcome with guilt?"

"He seemed totally fine and normal right up till he got sick," Imogen pointed out.

"What about the way he was acting at lunch?" I said. "Like he was drunk. Is that what happens if you shoot yourself up with insulin?"

Caleb shook his head. "Nick might know."

"It's how he'd act if he took my Xanax," Mandy said.

I pulled the now mostly empty purse closer to me and started checking the various compartments. "Lipstick. Tampon. Advil. Breath mints. Pen. Movie stub. A couple of receipts—groceries, drugstore. And—wait, what's this?" I pulled out a tightly folded piece of paper that had been tucked into the silky purse liner and smoothed it out. "It's a letter," I said, reading quickly. "Um, a love letter."

"From Warren?" Mandy asked. "That's so sad."

Caleb pushed in close to me and began reading aloud. "*Dear Claire, my perfect, beautiful Claire…*"

Imogen stuck her tongue out and made a gagging noise, and everyone shushed her.

"*It is amazing to me that there was ever a time I didn't know you,*" Caleb read. "*My feelings for you get stronger every day. No one has ever confided in me like you do and told me about all their feelings. I feel like we have both gone through so much and understand each other so much too. You are my moon and my stars and my sun…*"

"That last bit's e.e. cummings," I said. "Not even original. And it's not right either. It's supposed to be *my sun, my moon, and all my stars.*"

Caleb stopped reading and turned to me. "Seriously, Alice?"

"Sorry. You're right. Plagiarism isn't the point." I jabbed my finger at the end of the note. A name was scrawled there that I couldn't quite read, but it began with an *N*. "Actually, none of this slop is the point. *That* is. The signature." I looked around at the others. "The letter's not from Warren. Claire was having an affair. That's why she hid the letter."

Caleb studied the signature. "It's from Noah," he said. "Whoever that is."

There was a silence.

I knew I'd heard that name recently, but I couldn't remember where.

"Tara's boyfriend," Chad said. "Dude threw himself in front of a train, remember?"

"Oh my god, he's right." Imogen looked at me. "Claire was having a fling with Tara's boyfriend? That's…"

"Could be why she didn't want us encouraging Tara to find out who Noah was having an affair with," I said slowly. "Remember? Tara was talking about how she knew his passwords, how she was going to check his email when she got back home."

"And she never had the chance," Caleb said flatly.

"Noah was probably our age, right?" Imogen said. "I wonder how Claire met him."

"Tara said Noah was seeing a counselor," I reminded her.

Imogen nodded slowly. "Right. And if it got out that she'd had a relationship with a client, that'd be the end of her career."

"And her marriage," Mandy added. "Warren wouldn't have put up with that."

"I think she could go to jail," I said. "If he was underage and she was his counselor? That's a position of trust, right? Remember that teacher who had an affair with her student? It was all over the news. She got jail time."

"Well, there you have it," Chad said. "Claire must've killed Tara to shut that shit down."

"Killed her?" Mandy's hands flew to her face. "But I like Claire! And she was so nice to me!" she wailed. "About my pregnancy, I mean."

"You're pregnant?" Chad asked.

"She's not pregnant," I said. My mind was whirring, trying to put all the pieces into place. "After that first session, maybe Claire decided she couldn't risk Tara going home. She left her that note…"

"Signed my name," Caleb said bitterly.

"Because she figured Tara liked you," I told Caleb. "And she did."

He ducked his head but not fast enough to hide the glint of tears in his thick eyelashes.

"So Claire met Tara on the beach," Imogen said. "And what? Killed her somehow?"

It all sounded so farfetched.

"Probably stabbed her with a kitchen knife," Chad said. "Or sat her down on a log for a chat and came up behind her and hit her with a rock. Easy."

"There was blood on the log," I said.

We sat there for a few seconds, trying to take it in. I felt sick to my stomach, picturing the blood on the beach, imagining Tara lying there, dying.

I put the letter down. "Should we confront Claire? Or—"

"We don't know for sure," Caleb cut in. "I mean, it's not necessarily the same Noah."

"Some coincidence," I said, pushing aside a flicker of doubt.

"Granted, but coincidences do happen. And Warren could've killed himself." Caleb looked around at everyone. "To be honest, I agree. I think Claire did it. But we don't have solid proof."

"I think we should pretend not to know anything," Imogen said. "Like, don't spook her. Make her feel safe. Hang on until the boat comes on Saturday and then call the cops once we're safe."

Jason shook his head. "If she notices the safe is missing, we're screwed."

We all looked down at the evidence piled on the floor. "We could put it back," I said slowly. "Minus the evidence. As long as she didn't open it, she wouldn't know we'd found out."

"She would though," Mandy said. "To get her purse out."

Imogen nodded slowly. "You think it'd be better if she thought we'd taken the whole safe? She'd probably figure we couldn't open it."

"We can't put it back anyway. Not without getting her out of the staff cabin," Jason said. "Any ideas?"

I suddenly felt bone tired. "Maybe Mandy could fake another crisis."

"I don't want to be alone with her," Mandy protested. "Not if she's, like, a murderer."

"Wait, what about the insulin?" Imogen asked. "Did Claire use that to finish Tara off?"

I shook my head. "It disappeared later. Maybe she killed Warren with it."

"Why would she though?" Mandy said. "I mean, if she killed Tara to protect her marriage…"

"Maybe he found out," Jason suggested. "Or maybe Claire said it was an accident and Warren helped her get rid of the body, but she didn't trust him to keep his mouth shut. Or…"

"Doesn't matter," I said. "I mean, I want to know too, but we've got a bigger problem at the moment. We're pretty sure Claire's a psycho, and right now she's in the staff cabin with Rahim and Nick. What if she…" My words caught in my throat. "We have to warn Nick. Get him out of there." I looked around at the others. No one was jumping up to volunteer.

"Maybe we should confront her," Jason said. "All of us together."

"I don't know," I said. "If she was willing to kill to cover up an affair with a client, I don't suppose she'd be opposed to killing again to cover up a murder."

"It's one against seven," Jason pointed out.

"What if she has a gun?" I said.

Jason folded his arms across his chest. "If she had a gun, wouldn't she have used it on Tara?"

"Not if she wanted it to look like a suicide," I said.

There was a long silence. Caleb broke it. "Show of hands for confronting Claire tonight."

Jason's hand went up halfway.

"Show of hands for acting normal and waiting until tomorrow, at least."

The rest of us put up our hands.

"I'm going over to the staff cabin now though," I said. "To get Nick out of there."

"I'll go with you," Caleb said, getting to his feet.

"I'll be fine," I said.

Imogen laughed. "Let me guess—you're both oldest children, right?"

"Only child," Caleb and I said in unison, and everyone laughed.

"What?" I said, annoyed.

"Don't be mad." Imogen nudged me. "Just, you both like to be in charge, that's all. It's not a bad thing."

"I wasn't taking charge," Caleb said stiffly. "I thought we'd agreed no one would go anywhere alone."

I shook my head. "It'll be less suspicious if I go on my own, right? I'll pretend I have to talk to Nick about something personal."

"Lovers' quarrel?" Chad snorted. "You and Nick? Ha. Like that's believable."

I got to my feet and glared at him. "I wish Claire had cracked you on the head while she was at it."

"Not funny," Caleb said.

"Sorry." I stuck my hands in my pockets. "If I'm not back in ten minutes, come and find me."

"Five," Caleb said. "You've got five."

*   *   *

To my relief, when I knocked on the door to the staff cabin, it was Nick who opened it. "Alice. Hi."

"How's Rahim?"

Nick looked exhausted, with dark bruise-like circles under his eyes. "Not so good."

I could hear someone moving around in the master bedroom. Claire. I hoped to god she wouldn't look under her bed. "Can I talk to you?" I said loudly. "Privately? I had this fight with Imogen. I think she's breaking up with me."

"Oh shit, really?" He turned and called out, "Claire, I'm going outside with Alice for a few minutes. Can you watch Rahim?"

"No problem," Claire called back.

I shivered. She sounded so *normal.*

"Not that Rahim's going anywhere," Nick said, following me outside. "He's unconscious. I don't think he's going to make it until Saturday, Alice. We need to figure out some way to get help."

"Tell me about it," I said. I grabbed his arm, pulled him a few feet away from the cabin and, in a low voice, filled him in on everything that had happened. His eyes got wider and wider as he took it all in.

"Holy shit," he said when I finished. "Claire. Wow."

"You can't stay here," I said. "We're all going to sleep in the girls' cabin tonight. We'll barricade the door."

"What about Rahim?" Nick said.

I'd suspected he was going to say that. "It won't make a difference either way, will it?" I said. "I mean, he'll make it until Saturday or he won't."

Nick shook his head. "I'm not leaving him alone with a murderer. And if he wakes up—he's in and out—I want to be here for him."

"I don't want to leave you alone with a murderer either."

"She's got no reason to harm me. She's not just killing people for fun, is she? If you guys are right, she's all about damage control. Protecting her reputation. I'm not a threat to her. Besides, won't it make her more suspicious if I leave? I don't want to put everyone else at risk."

I opened my mouth to protest but stopped. He wasn't going to change his mind. "You're a good guy, Nick." I glanced at my watch. It had been four minutes. "I have to go," I told him. "Good luck."

He gave me a quick hug. "Look upset," he said. "In case Claire's watching out the window."

I put my head on his shoulder for a few seconds, faking tears. It wasn't hard—I was on the verge of collapsing into sobs for real. "Be careful, Nick," I said.

"Bye, Alice."

When I looked over my shoulder, he was still standing there, watching me walk away. He raised one hand in a wave, then turned, went back into the staff cabin and closed the door behind him.

FRIDAY

TWENTY-FIVE
Caleb

One more day.

One more night.

That's all we had to get through. Sounded simple. Until you factored in the whole bat-shit-crazy-killer scenario. Until you thought about Rahim, who wasn't going to last that long.

Everyone had survived the night, at least. Or I assumed we had. I still hadn't seen Nick. I had to believe that Claire hadn't offed him and Rahim in the night. Right now, as far as we knew, she had no idea we suspected her. Unless she'd gone looking for the safe or Nick had talked in his sleep or something. I wouldn't stop worrying until I'd seen both Nick and Rahim alive and well (or in Rahim's case, probably barely alive) with my own eyes. And it was only six in the morning. A bit early to do a bed check in the staff cabin.

I looked around at my fellow campers. Jason and I shouldn't have bothered hauling mattresses from the guys' cabin to the girls' cabin the night before. Imogen and Alice were cuddled up on Alice's bed under the INTRO blanket, their faces inches apart, sound asleep. Chad had convinced Mandy that she'd be safer if they shared her bunk. For once I was grateful that he was such an opportunistic douche. Mandy had had a very real panic attack when it got dark; even Imogen hadn't been able to help. It was only when Chad got up and took Mandy in his arms that she stopped shaking and crying. Male attention was the next best thing to Xanax, I guess. Spooning seemed like a logical next step. Score one for the Chadster.

Jason and I had taken turns on guard duty—two hours on, two hours off—even though we'd barricaded the door and shut all the windows. It was a long night. If Chad and Mandy had had sex, they'd been super stealthy. I wouldn't put it past them though. I just hoped they'd used a condom. Fake-pregnant Mandy was enough of a mess.

Now it was morning, and I was hungry.

I woke Jason up and together we moved the dresser away from the door. I snuck out of the cabin and ran to the mess hall, where I raided the kitchen for anything edible and portable. Bread, peanut butter, jam, bananas, apples, energy bars, juice and a few knives all went into an empty cardboard box. By the time I got back to the cabin, Jason had woken everybody up. It was time to make a war plan.

"I say we Rambo this shit up," Chad said, his mouth full of PB&J. "Take her down."

Alice and Imogen were sitting up under the blanket, sharing an energy bar. "Up, down. Which is it?" Alice said acidly. "And how exactly would we do that?"

"Bust into the cabin," Chad offered. "Take Claire by surprise. Tie her up. I dunno. You got something better?"

"Not really," Alice said. "But Nick's still in there. And Rahim, who can't exactly defend himself. We can't risk having them get hurt."

Chad grunted. "Yeah, Nick's not exactly built for battle. And Rahim's no use to anyone right now. Claire could probably take them both out, no problem."

"You're disgusting," Imogen said. "Nick's braver than any of us—the only one who's actually put himself in danger. In case you hadn't noticed, he spent the night *by choice* in the same cabin as a murderer. Didn't see you volunteering for that, did we, Rambo?"

"Someone had to stay here and look after the ladies," Chad said. "Right, Mandy?"

Mandy nodded and took a bite of an apple. "I guess." Of all of us, she looked the worst: blotchy skin, stringy hair (I could see where her extensions were coming loose), shadows under her eyes, cracked lips. Alice and Imogen, on the other hand, looked like Snow-White and Rose-Red in one of the books of fairy tales my mother had kept from her childhood. One blond, one dark; one slender, one curvy; both with rosy cheeks and red lips. I remembered something about a bear they looked after who turned out to be a prince. My mom loved fairy tales, even though her princes always turned out to be bears.

"I agree with Alice," I said. "Using force doesn't make sense. If we're right about everything, Claire's crazy, and she could be volatile. So we need to be smart. Get her away from the staff cabin without letting on that we know about Tara."

"How do you propose we do that?" Alice asked. "And what do we do with her once we get her alone?"

"We need to figure out her weakness," Jason said. "Then we exploit it. Once we get her out of the staff cabin, we lock her up in the guys' cabin until the boat comes. Piece of cake."

"That could work," I said. "But what's Claire's weakness?" I looked around at the others.

Alice laughed, but she didn't sound very happy. "Are you kidding me? It's pretty obvious, isn't it?" She looked from me to Jason to Chad. "She likes teenage boys. Troubled teenage boys. So which one of you is gonna volunteer?"

"She doesn't like me," Chad protested. "I tried already. Not damaged enough, I guess. So which one of you studs will it be?" He leered at Jason and me and grabbed his crotch. Mandy shuddered and moved away from him. I guessed even she had some standards.

"We don't really know that," I objected. "I mean, she had an affair with this guy Noah. Who may or may not have been Tara's Noah. But even if he was, that doesn't mean this is like a pattern for her." But even as I spoke, I remembered the way Claire had held my hand when she'd asked me to bury Warren.

"Uh…" Jason started to say something, then stopped.

Alice pounced on him. "What? Say it. Did she make a move on you?"

His face was a shade pinker than usual. "Maybe. Kind of flirted, like? I thought I was imagining it, but maybe I wasn't."

"You weren't," Imogen said. "So are you volunteering? Or do you want your turn, Caleb?"

Jason made a face and looked at me. "Flip you for it?" he asked. When I nodded, he dug in his pocket, pulled out a quarter and tossed it to Alice. "Call it," he said to me as we watched the coin turn in the air.

"Heads," I called.

"Tails," Alice said when the coin landed in her palm. She showed it to Imogen and then to us.

"Tails it is," I said. "But you're going to have to help me figure out what to do."

* * *

Half an hour later I was walking up the steps to the staff cabin, wearing one of Chad's Slayer T-shirts, which was at least two sizes too small for me. *You need more bicep action*, Mandy had said.

And try to look, you know, broody, Alice had added. *Angsty, not angry.*

I raised my hand to knock on the door. The mandatory biceps rippled under the tight shirt. I searched my soul for some angst. It wasn't hard to find. Just wearing a Slayer T-shirt made me question the meaning of life.

Nick answered the door, and I motioned to him to come outside.

"Is Claire still asleep?" I whispered as we stood on the steps.

Nick nodded. "She was up pretty late last night. Talking about Warren and all the stuff they had planned. Saying all the right things about Rahim, but there's something off there. Honestly, I don't think she gives a shit about him."

"How's he doing?"

"Bad." He hesitated. "Look, I was thinking: could we fix that kayak? Maybe I could paddle out and look for boats like Warren was supposed to do? I hardly know Rahim, but there's no way I'm letting the guy die."

"He's not gonna die," I said, more adamantly than I felt. What did I know about diabetic comas? "Can you hang in there with him for now?"

Nick nodded. "But I have to sleep. I've been awake all night. Can someone else come and be with him for a while? He needs to be woken up every couple of hours to drink, even if it's only a sip or two. I think keeping him hydrated is pretty much the only thing we can do."

"Okay, go to the girls' cabin and tell Imogen and Mandy to come stay with Rahim while you nap," I said.

"But you're going to have to sleep in there. We need the guys' cabin for something else."

As quickly as I could, I brought Nick up to speed on our plan.

"Well, beat as I am, I'm not sure I can sleep while that's going on. But at least it explains the shirt," he said when I was finished. "I was starting to worry about you. Didn't take you for a Slayer guy."

"I'm not. According to Mandy, it's all about the biceps," I said. "That and acting open and vulnerable. Which is a lot harder than it sounds."

He smiled wanly. "Any other day I'd appreciate the biceps. And the vulnerability. Right now I just want a nap."

"Soon, buddy, soon." I flexed my biceps and rippled my pecs. "Time to pull out the big guns."

"Good luck with that," he said. "I'll go wake her up and tell her you need her help." He hesitated, then met my eyes for a brief moment. "And watch your back, Caleb. Because if you guys are right about this? She's dangerous."

I waited on the steps, sitting with my head in my hands, the picture of despair. After about ten minutes the door opened, and Claire came out and sat down beside me. I didn't look up. She placed a hand on my arm. More accurately, on my bicep. I flexed gently. The hand stayed where it was.

"Caleb, what's wrong? Nick says he's worried about you."

She really didn't look dangerous. Not like a killer. Were we the crazy ones?

"I'm not sure I can talk about it," I said, doing my best to sound upset. It wasn't hard—my hands were cold and sweaty, and my stomach was in knots.

"Talk about what?"

I lifted my head and looked at her. Soulfully. "I'm so ashamed…"

"Of what, Caleb? You can tell me. This is a safe place."

I looked past her to the door of the cabin. "It's not," I said. "Nick is in there. We can't talk here."

"Where is the rest of the group?" she asked. "Still asleep?"

I shook my head. "They're at the mess hall. Eating breakfast. I feel too sick to eat."

"Anxiety will do that, Caleb," she said. "The last few days have been rough on everybody."

No kidding, I wanted to say. *Tara and Warren and Rahim would totally agree with that.*

"Feeling anxious is completely normal," she continued. "But most guys aren't brave enough to admit that they're not okay. I think I misjudged you, Caleb." Her hand stroked my arm. I tried not to flinch.

"There's no one in the guys' cabin," I said.

"Just let me grab my hoodie from my room." She disappeared into the staff cabin. A minute later she returned, pink hoodie over her arm, and held her hand out to me. I let her pull me to my feet and lead me down the path to the guys' cabin. It took all my willpower to keep my hand in hers. I wasn't kidding about feeling sick. When the door closed behind us, I could see her taking in the mess—clothes everywhere, mattresses on the floor, a pile of energy bars on Chad's bed and a stack of juice boxes on the floor, the half-closed blinds hanging over the open window.

"Boys," she said as she looked around. "So predictable."

She lowered herself to the edge of Jason's bunk and patted the mattress next to her. "Sit, Caleb. We can't talk with you looming over me."

I sat obediently, and she smiled at me. I suddenly understood what the expression "my flesh crawled" means. As unlikely as it seemed, I was almost certain this was a woman who had killed a girl to protect her job and her marriage…and then killed her husband too.

TWENTY-SIX
Caleb

"I'm glad you came to find me," she was saying. "Men are socialized to bottle up their emotions, but after everything that has happened, it's normal to feel overwhelmed. And it's healthy to share how you feel, Caleb—to want to connect with another person. Connection is a basic human need."

A phrase floated into my mind: *Incapable of feeling shame, guilt or remorse.* Where had that come from? And then I remembered. Before Barry, my mom had dated a total jerk named Norman. After they broke up, she was reading some magazine and came across an article about how to spot a sociopath. Norman was a textbook case. Smart, charming as hell, narcissistic and, yup, incapable of feeling shame, guilt or remorse.

Just like the woman next to me on the bed.

I moved away from her and stood up. "Is that what you told Noah?" I said as I moved toward the door. I spoke loudly so I wouldn't lose my nerve—and so that Jason, Chad and Alice, who should be waiting outside, could hear. "That all he needed was some *connection*? Did you tell him it was therapeutic?"

For a second she seemed frozen in place. Then she relaxed, smiling at me. "Caleb. *Noah*? Is this Tara's boyfriend you're talking about?" She shook her head. "Look, I don't know what Tara told you, but she wasn't...well, she was disturbed. She had trouble keeping track of what was real and what wasn't. I never met Noah. I didn't even meet Tara before this week."

I felt a flicker of uncertainty. If she was lying, she was disconcertingly good at it.

"We found the letter he wrote you," I said, then took a deep breath. "We know, Claire. You killed Tara to stop her from looking at Noah's emails. To make sure no one found out about your affair." There. It was out. I hoped to hell we were right.

Something changed in her face, like a shutter had lifted and I was suddenly seeing past the mask. Like she realized there was no point in continuing with the innocent act. Her eyes were cold, calculating—she was making a decision, I thought. Then the look was gone, so quickly I wondered if I had imagined it, and her eyes filled with tears. "Caleb...oh my god. You can't really think...you can't really believe..."

"I didn't want to," I said. "But the letter we found was pretty damning. And we found the empty insulin bottles and the radio part...Warren's dead and Rahim's dying, and none of *us* had access to the safe. So...well, it looks bad, Claire."

She pressed her fingers to her lips and shook her head, tears spilling out of her eyes.

"Why would you hide that stuff if you had done nothing wrong?" I asked.

She got to her feet and stepped closer. "Caleb. Listen to me."

Her voice was pleading and soft, her hand on my arm. I held my breath and forced myself to stay still. If she was about to confess, I didn't want to scare her off.

"Let me explain," she said. "I want you to understand, okay?"

I nodded. "I'm listening." I wished I had a recording device of some kind. It was too bad Jason hadn't known how to hack those phones.

"Noah was a client in my counseling practice. In Vancouver. This was a couple of years ago now. And he and I, well…we fell in love. Deeply in love." She looked up at me through long wet lashes. "Have you ever been in love, Caleb?"

I ignored her question. "How old was he?" I asked. "Fifteen? Sixteen?"

"That's not the *point*, Caleb." Her voice rose a little. "The point is, we were in love. He was young, and he was my client, and I was married. But we couldn't let those things come between us, not when we felt the way we did about each other. We had no choice but to keep our relationship a secret."

"And then…what, he killed himself?"

Claire flinched, closing her eyes for a second. "It was awful, Caleb. You can't imagine how I felt when I heard the news. I'd tried so hard to help him." She slid her hand down my arm and squeezed my wrist. "And, of course, I had to carry on as if nothing was wrong. I had to grieve in silence."

I pulled my hand away. "So when Tara started talking about her boyfriend killing himself—is that when you realized?"

She nodded. "I'd had no idea who she was. But when she said her boyfriend was called Noah, and she talked about how he'd died, I knew it must be her."

"And we were all telling her to check his email, find out who he'd been involved with..." I trailed off. If we hadn't done that, would Tara still be here?

"I didn't have a choice," Claire said. "You can see that, can't you? I couldn't let Tara go home and start snooping around. I would've lost everything. My marriage, my counseling practice, INTRO. All of it."

"So you killed her?" I knew the answer, but I wanted to hear her say it.

"I had no choice," she repeated. "Caleb, you have to understand. Noah was damaged. I loved him, but he was never going to be okay. And Tara was the same. Weak. Pathetic, really. She'd probably have ended up killing herself anyway. But I...well, I have my whole future ahead of me. I have so much *good* I can do." Her eyes met mine. "I can help people, Caleb. I've trained for years to be able to help people, and I am excellent at my job. Should that all go to waste because of one little mistake? It didn't make sense."

"You signed my name," I said. "You left her a note, and you signed my name. And you met her on the beach and… then what?"

"She didn't see it coming," Claire said. Her face was close to mine, her gaze intense. "She didn't suffer at all. I want you to know that, Caleb, because I can see you're a deeply compassionate person. I am too. I didn't want to do this, you know? It's just the way things turned out."

"What did you do to her?" My voice cracked.

"She was sitting on the log, waiting for me. Well—for you, I suppose." She smiled up at me like this was somehow amusing. "And then I…snuck up behind her. I had a large rock. And I hit her with it. It was that easy."

I took a step backward, unable to bear her face being so close to mine. "Right. Easy. And the…her body…"

"I told Warren there'd been an accident. I told him Tara met me on the beach to talk and that she slipped and hit her head. He was so upset. He actually cried. He wanted to report it right away." She bit her bottom lip and looked off to one side, as if she was remembering it. "I couldn't let him do that. We'd lose INTRO if a camper died in an accident— parents wouldn't trust us to keep their kids safe. So I told him I was scared I'd be blamed for it. Since I was with her when it happened. Warren hated to see me cry; he always wanted to protect me. And since Tara was dead anyway, and me getting in trouble wouldn't bring her back…" She brushed her hands together like a little kid signing *all done*. "He put her body in one kayak and pulled it out to sea with the other one."

I nodded, trying to keep my face blank, my expression neutral. I couldn't believe she was telling me all this. Talking about it like it was all reasonable. Sensible. Like she'd had no other option. Did she really see it that way? "And then— what about Warren?" I asked. "What happened to him?"

She sighed. "He had a crisis of conscience and wanted to call the police," she said. "To report the accident. I smashed the radio and sliced up the other kayak to buy some time, to talk him around, to make him see reason…but he wouldn't let it go."

"So you…what, dosed him with Xanax somehow and injected him with insulin once he passed out?" I shook my head. "Claire, you can't honestly think you're going to walk away from this. I mean, you've just confessed to two cold-blooded murders."

"Who's to say Warren didn't inject himself? Or take a fatal overdose of Xanax? And you can claim I confessed if you want, but look at you. A teenager with a history of assault." She raised her eyebrows. "And look at me. Who's going to believe a bunch of drug-addled teenage criminals over a psychologist? Believe me, if you even *try* to pin this on me, you'll be the one going down for murder."

"No way." I clenched my fists, my nails digging into my palms. "Not a chance."

"We'll see." She laughed. "Don't forget Warren was a cop. He has lots of cop friends who will be only too happy to console his grieving widow. And I'll have another bunch of morons out here next month. There's no shortage of parents desperate to pay good money to rehabilitate their precious darlings. This camp is a gold mine. And my work is getting me a lot of attention. I wasn't about to lose that." She tossed her hoodie on to the bed behind her. "And I'm not going to let you tell your friends and take everything away from me either."

Claire lunged at me. God, where did that knife come from? It must've been in her hoodie pocket. She must have guessed we knew something.

"She has a knife!" I yelled, dodging to one side.

Claire came after me, lips pulled back from her teeth in a hideous grin. I was twice her size, but she was wild, and she was holding the knife in front of her. To get close, I'd have to risk getting cut.

I could hear Jason outside the door, fumbling with the door handle. "Hurry!" I shouted, trying to catch Claire's wrist. The knife sliced into the fleshy part of my hand, right below my thumb. "Shit! Guys…" I dodged again, backing away from her, backing myself into a corner—and then the door flew open, and Alice came flying through it.

One perfectly aimed roundhouse kick was followed by a lightning-quick elbow strike. It was fast, it was precise and, man, was it effective. In a few seconds Claire was on the floor, writhing and moaning, with blood pouring out of her nose.

"Jesus," Jason said. He kicked the knife away and then picked it up gingerly, using his sleeve to avoid leaving finger-prints. "What was *that*?"

"I told you I had a black belt in karate," Alice said, her voice trembling slightly. She had her knee on Claire's back. "Tie her hands," she said.

Jason picked up the coil of rope we'd retrieved from one of the sheds earlier. I hadn't thought we'd need it—the idea of tying Claire up had seemed ludicrous. Melodramatic. Now it was unavoidable, and I was glad he'd insisted on bringing the rope despite my misgivings.

Jason pulled Claire's wrists behind her back and tied them together tightly. Then he got to work on her ankles. Chad stood watching, shaking his head like he couldn't quite believe any of this was real.

"That was awesome, Alice," I said. "I'd hug you if we weren't in the same room with a psycho killer. And if I wasn't bleeding everywhere." I pressed my hand against my side. Chad was going to be pissed when he noticed the mess I'd made of his Slayer shirt.

She got to her feet, smiling slightly. "You wouldn't be scared of getting kicked yourself?"

I just shook my head. "That was pretty damn impressive."

Alice closed the window, and we slipped out the door, leaving Claire shouting and swearing on the floor behind us. Outside the cabin, Jason, Alice and Chad had assembled a pile of wood and tools, ready to nail a two-by-four across the door. We could hear Claire kicking frantically with her bound feet.

"You okay, mate?" Jason asked as he hammered the nails into place. "You look like shit."

"Maybe it's the T-shirt," I said.

"You did great in there. We could hear most of it. That was some crazy shit."

"Tell me about it."

"I'll stay here while you go change. Then someone should tell Mandy and Imogen—they're still with Rahim. Nick's out cold. Slept through all the excitement." He hammered the last nail and brushed his hands together. "There. Claire's not going anywhere. It's all good."

"I'll feel better once she's in a real jail," I said.

But her words were still ringing in my head. *If you even try to pin this on me, you'll be the one going down for murder.*

TWENTY-SEVEN
Alice

I stood at the beach, ankle deep in the waves, eyes on the horizon. It was midafternoon, the sun high in the hazy gray sky. Claire was tied up and locked in the guys' cabin, and Chad was guarding her. Imogen and Mandy were still watching Rahim, who was unconscious, his heart racing and his breathing shallow.

And Caleb and I were about to paddle out to sea in a badly repaired, leaking kayak. Jason and Nick had done their best with some duct tape they'd found in one of the outbuildings, but the kayak looked pretty shaky to me. There were several long slashes in the plastic, and in one place a large jagged hole had been cut. I knew duct tape was great stuff, but now we'd be betting our lives on its seaworthiness.

"Be safe out there," Jason said from the beach. "Don't go too far. I don't know how well the boat'll hold up."

Wordlessly, Nick handed me the manual pump. He nodded, and I saw his Adam's apple jump as he swallowed.

"Ready?" Caleb said.

"As I'm ever going to be," I said, and I stepped into the kayak behind him.

Here was the plan. Caleb was going to paddle. I was going to pump out any water that breached the duct tape. Some helpful boater was going to sail by, stop to say hello and call for help on the radio.

It was crazy, but it was the only hope for Rahim.

Nick and Jason helped push us off, the bottom of the boat briefly grinding against the rocks. Then they stood on the beach, watching silently as Caleb dipped the paddle into the water, and we were away, leaving the island behind us.

Neither of us spoke much. I couldn't stop replaying the moment when Caleb had yelled that Claire had a knife. Jason fumbling with the door handle in a panic, me flying into the room and taking her out. I'd never done anything like that before. Karate was a sport, and I was good at it. But for me, it had always been about learning katas and going to classes at the dojo and competing in tournaments. Actually hitting a person, with the intent to take them down? Not a chance.

I shook for an hour.

Now I pumped—amazingly, not much water was coming in. Yet. All good until the salt water unstuck the duct tape, I guessed.

Caleb paddled, the blades dipping and curving through the water in a smooth figure eight.

And we scanned the horizon. What the hell were we going to do if no boats showed up? I imagined paddling back, telling the others we'd been unsuccessful. Imagined watching Rahim die.

We'd been out there for over two hours when I spotted the white triangle of a sail in the distance.

Thank God.

"Look! Caleb! Over there!"

Caleb nodded grimly. His hand was bandaged, but blood was seeping through. He probably should've stayed and guarded Claire and let Chad or Jason paddle, but he'd insisted on doing this himself.

I waved frantically and shouted until I was hoarse. The sailboat stayed within sight for half an hour maybe, teasing us with faint hope—and then sailed right on past and vanished. It never came anywhere near us.

"We're hard to spot," Caleb said. He stopped paddling and turned to look at me. "A tiny kayak, flat against the water? We should have flares or something."

"Yeah, well, we don't." I pumped. Water was coming in steadily, but so far I could keep up with it. My running shoes were soaked, though, and my feet were frozen. "So keep going."

Caleb hesitated. "Alice."

I knew what he was going to say. "No," I said. "We can't give up. If we do, Rahim dies. It's that simple."

"I don't want to risk you dying too," he said. "Or me, to be honest. I mean, at what point do we quit? When this piece-of-shit kayak sinks?"

Our eyes met, and for a moment neither of us spoke. I couldn't hold back a shiver. "Five more minutes," I said. "Then we turn around."

Caleb nodded. "Five more minutes."

In the third minute, we heard the roar of an outboard engine.

In the fourth minute, we saw the Zodiac.

And in the fifth, Del was pulling up alongside, empty crab traps piled high in his boat. "Hey, it's the goddamn delinquents! Are you kids trying to run away?" He pulled out his radio. "Can't let you do that. I'm calling Warren."

"Warren's dead," I told him. And then—to my absolute shame and fury—I burst into tears.

TWENTY-EIGHT

Alice

It wasn't until we were back on the island, helping Del get the Zodiac secured to the dock, that I realized he hadn't believed me.

"Okay, where's Warren?" he demanded.

I stared at him.

"Drop the act, will you? Where is he?" A cigarette dangled from his lip, and his eyes were shaded by a new-looking bright-green baseball cap. It said *I'm not a doctor, but I'll take a look.*

Charming.

"Warren's dead," Caleb said. "Like she told you."

"Tara's dead too. And Rahim's really sick," I put in. "Can you call the police? On your radio?"

"Come on, sweetie." He took his cigarette out of his mouth. "That's not funny."

"I'm not kidding," I said. "Claire killed him. You should call the paramedics too—get an ambulance to meet us.

Rahim's insulin disappeared a few days ago, and he's in terrible shape. Come and see for yourself if you don't believe me."

Caleb and I started to run up the path, gesturing for him to follow us.

He didn't move. "Listen, kids. I don't have time for this."

I turned back to face him. "We're not kidding. I *wish* we were kidding, okay? We've got all kinds of evidence. And Rahim is, like, in a coma or something…"

Del dropped his cigarette butt and ground it out with his heel. "All right, all right. I'm coming." He glared at me. "To talk to one of the *adults*."

Jason and Mandy came running down the path when they spotted us.

"Chad's guarding Claire," Jason said. "Imogen and Nick are with Rahim." He looked at Del. "Have you called the cops? Rahim needs to be in a hospital. Like, two days ago."

"Where are Claire and Warren?" Del asked. He hooked his thumb through a belt loop and stood there stubbornly.

Jason looked at me. "Didn't you tell him?"

"I told him."

There was a brief silence, and then Jason said, "Oh, come *on*. You don't believe us? Why would we make this up?"

Del shrugged. "You're all, uh, troubled teens, right? No offense."

Mandy folded her arms across her chest, looking decidedly offended.

"Come take a look at Rahim first," Jason said.

* * *

Nick and Imogen jumped up when we walked in.

"You got help!" Imogen threw her arms around me and hugged me tightly. "I was so scared!"

"How is he?" I asked.

"Listen to his breathing," Nick said. "It sounds awful."

It did. It was deep and gasping and kind of desperate-sounding.

At any rate, it was enough to get Del jogging back down the hill to the Zodiac to make a call from his radio. When he returned, he was breathing hard—I had the feeling he wasn't someone who made a habit of running. "Paramedics are gonna meet us at the dock on the mainland," he said between huffs. "Get him to a hospital."

I hoped it wasn't too late.

"Now, where's Claire?" Del asked. "I need to talk to her."

Jason's eyes met mine. "Uh, she's in the guys' cabin," I said. "Locked in."

Del bristled. "You locked her in? Well, I'm putting a stop to this right now. That poor girl."

Nick stayed with Rahim, and the rest of us headed over to the guys' cabin.

Chad waved at us as we approached. "Hey, Del. Man, are we ever glad to see you."

"He wants to talk to Claire," I said.

Chad grunted. "Well, we have to bring her out sometime, right? We're all leaving here together." He pried the board off the front door and pulled the door open. "Come on, Claire. Time to go."

* * *

Naturally, Del was kind of primed to take Claire's side.

Her tight-fitting T-shirt probably didn't hurt either. Nor did the fact that as soon as he had her untied, she threw her arms around him and said, "Oh, Del! Thank God you're here."

Like he was her knight in shining armor.

Del patted her back awkwardly. "It'll be okay," he said. "It's all going to be okay. Hey…" He touched her cheekbone, which had turned a gruesome shade of puce. "What happened here? Did one of these boys hurt you?"

Claire scowled and looked at me. "That girl attacked me."

"Because she was attacking Caleb!" I said. "With a knife! Not to mention that she's killed two people—"

Del took a step back and lit a cigarette. "The kids said that Warren was dead. They're screwing with me, right?"

Claire wiped away a tear. "I think it was food poisoning— or a heart attack. He wasn't feeling well, and he went to lie down…and he never woke up."

"Oh man." Del exhaled a cloud of smoke. "I mean, shit. That's…I'm so sorry, Claire. Warren's dead? Man." He shook his head slowly. "He was good people."

Claire bit her bottom lip. "And a girl ran away, and they think—they *accused* me—"

Caleb cut her off. "Look, Del. Just call the cops, okay? I don't care whether you believe she's a killer or that a bunch of delinquents attacked her and locked her in a cabin. Either way, you gotta call for help."

"And we have to leave—fast," I said. "Because Rahim is *dying*."

Del looked at me, then at Caleb and then at Claire. None of us said anything. He scratched his stomach, adjusted the brim of his baseball cap. "Right," he said. "You three"—he nodded at Caleb, Chad and Jason—"go help that other boy carry Rahim down to the dock. You girls, get your little butts into the Zodiac. Pronto."

"What about our clothes and stuff?" Mandy asked.

"Seriously, Mandy?" I said.

The only thing we needed to bring was Claire's purse and the evidence inside it—and that was still in the girls' cabin. I didn't want to mention it in front of Claire and Del. I ran a few steps after Caleb, who was already jogging toward the staff cabin. "Caleb!"

"Pronto!" Del yelled. Claire hung on to his arm and murmured something.

Caleb turned back toward me.

"Get her purse," I whispered.

He nodded. "On it."

Del reached out to grab me. "Listen, little lady. If your pretty little backside isn't in that Zodiac in sixty seconds flat, you're going to be very sorry. Now move it."

I yanked my arm free. "Fine!" I was in as much of a hurry to get out of there as anyone, so I ran down to the Zodiac, Mandy and Imogen close on my heels.

Del and Claire followed us, and a minute later the boys were making their way down the slope. Nick and Jason were carrying Rahim—Nick had his arms locked under Rahim's, with Rahim's back and head supported against his chest, and Jason was in front, holding up Rahim's legs. Right behind them was Caleb. To my relief, he had a duffel bag slung over one shoulder.

Del drove at top speed, the Zodiac pounding against the chop. I could hear him talking to the police dispatcher on the radio. Sounded like the cops would be meeting us at the dock as well as the paramedics. I just wasn't sure who was going to be getting arrested.

Rahim lay on a pile of blankets. He looked like he was already dead. He even smelled strange. He was still doing that weird breathing. It didn't seem like a good sign to me, but it was better than not breathing at all. Nick was crouched down beside him, his jaw clenched. He looked scared, and that made me even more frightened. We were so close to getting medical help—but what if it was too late?

Claire sat beside Del at the back of the boat. In snatches, I could hear her explaining it all away, shouting her lies over the noise of the engine and the wind like she could erase the truth with her bullshit stories. What I was hearing was enough to ratchet up my anxiety by a few more degrees.

"I don't blame the kids, Del," she was yelling. "They came here because they have problems. Difficulty accepting reality. Poor coping skills. And this was an extraordinarily stressful situation. It isn't surprising that they would panic and overreact."

"You're being awful understanding," Del shouted back. "Those brats locked me up? I'd be pissed."

"It's my job to understand them," Claire yelled.

Imogen grabbed my arm. "I think I'm gonna be sick."

"No kidding," I said. "Me too."

"No, I mean—" She pushed past me, leaned over the side of the boat and vomited.

Caleb swiveled around on his seat in front of us. "She's seasick again?"

I nodded, rubbing Imogen's back. "Did you hear that, Caleb? What Claire was saying to Del?"

"No. Too noisy."

"It was all about how the disturbed teens panicked and locked her up. Del obviously believes every word she's saying. What if the cops do too?"

Caleb nudged the large duffel bag between his feet. "We've got the evidence on our side, right? The love letter, the insulin bottles. They can't ignore that."

Imogen sat up and wiped her mouth on her sleeve. "Oh my god, I feel like I'm dying here." She turned away from us suddenly and leaned over the side of the Zodiac again, dry-heaving.

Nick was still kneeling beside Rahim.

"You think he's going to make it?" Caleb asked, his mouth close to my ear.

"I don't know anything about it," I said. "I mean, maybe if he gets insulin, he gets better? I hope so."

"He was a decent guy," Caleb said.

The way he said it—in past tense—told me what he thought.

"Why did we wait so long to take the kayak out?" My voice wobbled. "We should've gone for help days ago."

I knew why we hadn't though. We'd been thinking the adults would take care of things. It wasn't until Warren was dead, Rahim unconscious and Claire locked up that we'd realized it was up to us.

TWENTY-NINE
Alice

An ambulance and several cop cars were waiting at the dock when we arrived. The paramedics loaded Rahim into the back of the ambulance and peeled out, sirens blaring. I watched the ambulance disappear around the corner and tried to ignore the ache in my throat.

Claire acted like the police were there at her personal request, shaking hands with them and introducing herself as Dr. Addison. I could hear her fervent thank-you to each of them.

The police directed Del and Claire to get into a waiting police car. "And you kids, into the van. We'll need statements from all of you," a round-faced female officer told us.

"I should warn you, several of these kids are addicts. You won't get a true word from any of them," Claire said to the male officer standing beside the car. "Alice, for example, has a tendency to…well, to tell lies. Alcoholics often confabulate to cover up the memory gaps from their blackouts."

"I'm not an alcoholic," I snapped.

"Tell Officer Nichols why you were at INTRO," Claire chided. "It's right on the intake forms your mother filled out."

Officer Nichols? She already knew all their names? "I had a few drinks at a party," I said. "That's all. Why are we talking about me? It's not like *I* killed anyone."

"All right, simmer down," the female officer said. "There'll be plenty of time for you to tell us your version of things at the station."

"Our version?" Imogen said. She'd regained her composure once we were back on dry land. "It's not our version. It's the truth. And we have evidence."

"Evidence?" Claire gave a sad laugh and shook her head. "It's just too awful. Having a girl go missing, losing my husband...and then having the other kids all gang up and turn on me like that." She wiped a tear from her cheek. "I can't believe this is all happening."

"Cue the violin music," I said.

A male officer with a neat mustache turned his head to look at me. "She just lost her husband," he said, sounding shocked at my callousness. "Have a little respect."

"She just *killed* her husband," I retorted. "And Tara. You want me to have some respect? I don't think so."

"That's *enough*, Alice," Officer Nichols said. "Not another word until we get to the station."

"Thank you, Officer," Claire said, her voice shaking. "I appreciate that."

"We have a Victim Services office at the station," the male officer told her. "We'll make sure you get taken care of." He put a hand on Claire's arm. "Here, let's get you into the car…"

My hands got really cold all of a sudden, and a tingling shot down my arms—that same feeling I get when I have stage fright at a karate tournament. Adrenaline, I guess.

Was Claire actually going to get away with this?

The guys filed into the van. I hung back with Mandy and Imogen.

The police officer beckoned us over to the van. "You three. In here with the boys," she ordered.

"Group hug," I said loudly, putting my arms around Imogen and Mandy. "I bet they split us up at the station," I whispered. "You don't have to talk to them, you know. We have a right to have our parents present if they're going to be questioning us."

"Do we need a lawyer?" Mandy sounded frightened.

"I don't see why *we* should need one," I said. "We've done nothing wrong. But wait until your mom comes before you talk to them. And don't sign anything."

"Right now," the officer said. "Let's go. I'm not asking again." She held the back door of the van open, and I slid in beside Caleb.

* * *

None of us spoke much in the van. For one thing, the police could hear everything we said. For another, we were all too nervous. Chad's arm around Mandy's shoulders was the only thing keeping her from completely losing it. Imogen was hunched up and withdrawn. Nick's jaw was clenched so tightly I could see a muscle twitching beneath the skin. Jason had his knees pulled up in front of him and his face buried in his arms. For him, and for Chad and Caleb, this was not the first brush with the police. The three of them were probably scared shitless about what would happen to them if the cops believed Claire. I mean, we'd locked her in a cabin overnight. What was that? Unlawful confinement or something?

Then Caleb nudged me, and when I looked up at him, he gave me a tiny nod. Just a small dip of his chin like, *Hang in there*. But it made me feel better.

They split us up when we arrived at the station. I was whisked off to some tiny room and left there. After what seemed like an hour, the female officer from the van came in with a coffee in one hand and a clipboard in the other.

"We're taking statements from everyone who was on the island," she said. "I need you to sign this waiver. It simply says you agree to talk to us. Then I'll ask you a series of questions, and—"

I cut her off. "I want to call my mother," I said. "I'll make a statement once she gets here."

She sighed. "Really, Alice? No one is accusing you of anything. We're just trying to understand what happened."

"Claire was accusing me," I said. "You heard her."

She sighed again and nodded. "Fine. Call your mother."

* * *

Mom was shocked to hear from me, obviously—I was supposed to be In Nature Renewing Myself, not in some random police station—but after a few rapid-fire questions, she told me she was on her way. "Sit tight till I get there," she said. "And don't sign anything."

It took her less than two hours to drive up to the Sunshine Coast from Vancouver, though it felt like forever. I spent the time going around and around in circles—reviewing the evidence in my mind, worrying about how persuasive Claire could be, wondering how Rahim was doing at the hospital and whether he was going to survive.

When my mom arrived she was out of breath, as if she'd sprinted the whole way on foot. She gave me a rib-crushing hug and then released me.

"I'd like a few minutes alone with my daughter," she told the police officer, who nodded and left us alone.

"Tell me," my mom said.

And I told her everything. About what Tara had said in group and her disappearance that night, about the missing kayak and the frantic search, and about the blood on the beach. I told her about Warren getting sick after he ate the lunch Caleb and I made, and about the announcement the next morning that he was dead. I told her about the guys burying Warren in the woods, and about the missing insulin, and about Rahim getting ill and Nick taking care of him. I told her about the safe and all the evidence we had tried to preserve as well as we could, and about Claire attacking Caleb and me kicking her in the head and all of us locking her up.

I even told her about Imogen and me. Which, crazy as it might sound, was the part I was most nervous about.

When I was done, my mom just sat there for a long time, biting her lip, studying my face, taking it all in. "And that's it? Nothing else?"

"That's it."

She met my eyes directly. "Alice, this is important. Is there anything you've left out? Anything that…that you could get in trouble for?"

"Other than kicking Claire in the head?"

"Anything at all."

I shook my head. "I told you everything."

I could see her relax. Then she said, "Okay. You did good, kiddo." She glanced down at her watch. "Remember my friend Alexis?"

"Uh, red hair? Swimmer, right?"

"She also happens to be a lawyer. And she's on her way. You can tell all of this to her, and she'll stay with you when you make a statement to the police. She'll make sure your rights are protected."

I thought of Caleb and the others, who probably didn't have lawyers looking out for them. "What if the police think we're lying? What if they believe Claire?"

She shook her head. "Just tell them what happened. There are seven of you telling the truth, and only one lying. And believe it or not, sorting through statements and evidence and sifting out the facts is something detectives aren't too bad at."

"Okay," I said.

She grinned at me. "Maybe skip the part about your girlfriend. That's none of their business."

*　　*　　*

My mom's lawyer friend was a large woman with a reassuringly businesslike manner. After I'd spoken with her and made my statement to the police, I was told I could leave with my mother. "Has Claire been arrested?" I asked. "Are you charging her?"

"I'm afraid I can't give you any information at this time," the officer said. She glanced at my mom. "We took statements from all the campers. There will be a full investigation, and the physical evidence from the safe and the island will need to be analyzed. The Integrated Homicide team will look at the young man's—Noah's—emails and see if those corroborate the kids' story. There will need to be an autopsy of Warren's body, obviously. And there's Caleb's injury—we've photographed it, but they'll have to find the knife and check it for fingerprints. The whole island's basically a crime scene."

Tell me about it, I thought.

The officer turned to me. "Don't leave Vancouver. The detectives may need to talk to you further."

"You're not letting Claire go, are you?" I said.

She hesitated. "Like I said, I can't really give you any information, but…" She looked at my mother and then back at me. "No. No, she isn't going anywhere right now."

As we walked out of the police station, my mom took my hand and gave it a squeeze. "I'm proud of you, Alice," she said.

I stiffened a little but didn't let go of her hand. "So does that mean you admit you shouldn't have sent me there?"

"I think that's obvious. My *god*, Alice. I had no idea Warren's wife—"

I cut her off. "Not that. I mean, that I didn't need to go to any stupid—"

"Oh, honey." She released my hand, stopped walking and turned to face me, right there in the middle of the parking lot. "I was worried. You know that. I was trying to do the right thing."

I had a sudden lump in my throat, and it took an effort to keep my voice steady. "I know."

"You're angry though?"

I didn't answer right away. I didn't know how I felt. Mostly I just felt exhausted. "I was," I said. "But maybe not so much anymore."

Mom pulled her keys out of her purse as we neared our Subaru. "Well, I'm not about to send you away again after—" She stopped mid-sentence. "Is that one of your friends?"

I looked where she was pointing. Caleb was sitting on a sidewalk bench outside the entrance to the cop shop. "Hey," I called. "Caleb?"

He stood up and walked toward us. "Hi, Alice. And, uh, Mrs....or is it Detective?"

"It's Diane. Hi." My mom held out a hand, and Caleb shook it.

"How did it go?" I asked him.

He shrugged. "Hard to tell. I gave them all the evidence. Told them what I knew."

"What are you doing sitting out here?" I asked him. "Your mom...is she here?"

He shook his head. "She's not coming."

"What? That's..." I trailed off. No point in saying how lousy it was—it'd only make him feel worse. "What are you going to do?"

"Take a bus back to Vancouver, I guess."

"Do you have somewhere to go? I mean, you can't go home, right? Not with your stepfather there."

He brushed something invisible off his sleeve. "Don't worry about me. I'll figure something out."

I looked at my mom. Just a look. She knew. "Caleb," she said, "we're driving back to the city. No point in you taking the bus when we have plenty of room in the car. Why don't you come with us?"

"Yeah? That'd be awesome." He grinned. "Thanks."

So Caleb and I got into the car together, and my mom broke the speed limit all the way home.

THREE
MONTHS
LATER

THIRTY
Caleb

I came out of my room when I heard the doorbell ring. It still felt weird—going up the stairs from the basement into Rahim's tidy kitchen. I couldn't quite get my head around the fact that I had a home—a good home—and a foster father. I had spent the first few weeks after leaving INTRO at Alice's house, and her mom, Diane, had helped me navigate the legal system, since my own mom had declined to lift a finger to help me. Apparently Barry had given her an ultimatum—him or me—and guess who she chose? I should probably get some help processing that shit, but let's just say I'm a bit wary of therapists these days. Except for Rahim. He's cool.

As soon as he had recovered enough to pick up a phone, he had called all of us to make sure we were okay. When he found out what was going on in my life, he offered to be my court-appointed guardian until he was approved as my foster parent. I still don't really know why. He said it was because he saw potential in me and because he had a spare room in his basement. This sounds sappy, but I think it was because he had extra room in his heart. I've been here nearly two months now. I've got my own entrance and my own bathroom. I help out around the house, not only because Rahim is still a bit weak from his near-death experience, but because I want to.

"I'll get the door," I told Rahim, who was taking some mini-quiches out of the oven.

Nick and Jason were standing on the doorstep, laughing about something. I hadn't seen them since the day we left the island, but we'd talked on the phone a few times, keeping each other up-to-date on life after INTRO.

Nick was carrying a plastic tray of cupcakes; Jason handed me a giant bag of chips and a huge bottle of hot salsa. We headed for the kitchen.

"Anyone else here yet?" Jason asked.

"Nope. You're the first. Mandy's not coming—her folks sent her to some clinic in New Hampshire."

"No Mandy?" Nick said. "Who will Chad hit on?"

"No Chad either," I said. "He's MIA. I texted him and left messages. Nothing."

"Can't say that breaks my heart," Jason said. "Guy's an idiot."

"But he's *our* idiot," Nick said. "He should be here."

"I agree," Rahim said. We followed him into the living room, where he put the tray of quiches on the coffee table. "But it's great to see you two. Nick, how are things with your parents?"

"Better after you talked to them," Nick said.

"Somebody had to tell them that their son saved my life," Rahim said. "And I may have had a few things to say about how brave you were, and how selfless. I also may have talked a bit about their, uh, misguided beliefs."

"Their homophobia, you mean," Nick said. He turned to us. "Rahim read them the riot act. It was awesome."

"So it's all fine now?" Jason asked.

"Well, it's better," Nick said. "Not perfect. I can see my dad struggling, but my mom's been great. She keeps asking me if I want to go shopping with her, like that's a gay thing."

"Isn't it?" Jason asked.

Nick punched him in the shoulder. "Imogen and Alice are coming, right?" he said.

As if on cue, the doorbell rang, and there they were, holding hands and beaming.

"Well, that's one question answered," Nick said, hugging first Alice and then Imogen.

"What question is that?" Alice asked.

"Whether you and Imogen are still together."

Alice giggled and blushed. They were pretty cute together, I had to admit.

Rahim joined us, wiping his hands on an apron that said *The last time I cooked, hardly anyone got sick.* A little ghoulish, under the circumstances, but funny.

He kissed Alice and Imogen on both cheeks, European-style. "There's plenty of food, and there's a cooler full of drinks in the kitchen. Nonalcoholic, of course. Help yourselves."

We stuffed ourselves and talked for a while—small talk, mostly, everyone acting like this was a normal kind of get-together and not a postmurder reunion.

Nick and I were loading the dishes into the dishwasher when the doorbell rang again. I heard Rahim say, "This is a welcome surprise," and a few minutes later Alice barreled into the kitchen, closely followed by Imogen.

"It's Chad," Alice hissed. "Can you believe it?"

"And he's high," Imogen added. "I can smell weed on him. Good thing we ate most of the food already."

Jason stuck his head into the kitchen. "Help me out here, guys. Chad's off his face, and he's all weepy. Wants to talk about INTRO, if you can believe it."

We straggled back into the living room, where Chad had already installed himself on the couch. "It was so heavy, man," he was saying to Rahim. "I can't deal."

Rahim nodded. "It was tough for all of us, but we have to move forward." He cleared his throat. "I assume none of you have seen Claire since you were at the police station."

We looked at each other and shook our heads.

"My mom says she's in jail," Alice said. "Where she belongs."

"That's right," Rahim said. "She's been charged with two murders and attempted murder. No bail. Trial's a long way off, but you may all be asked to testify. I'll be with you every step of the way. You can call me anytime, talk about anything, okay? It's a difficult path we've been on, but it's an honor to travel it with you."

Everybody nodded, and I noticed Alice suppressing a smile.

"And now let's talk about what's going on in your lives," Rahim said. "Jason, I think you have some news?"

"Yeah," Jason said. "I'm quitting the family business. Going straight. I'm going to be a locksmith." He chuckled. "Put my talents to good use, right?" He looked down at his hands. "My da and my brothers are pissed, but my sister's been awesome. And my mom wants to pay for the course, even if Da doesn't like it."

"That's amazing," I said. I didn't want to tell them that my mom had all but washed her hands of me, so I said, "Hey, I have something I want to show you—something I made for Tara's grandmother. I guess you all know Tara's body was finally found by a fishing boat up the coast? And her grandmother is having a private funeral?"

Everyone nodded.

"Uh, so…" I hesitated. Cleared my throat. "So I drew a portrait of Tara for her, and I'd like you all to sign it. If that's okay."

I pulled the portrait from behind a bookshelf, looked at it for a long moment, then leaned it on the mantel.

"It's not perfect," I said. "I did it from memory." I had drawn Tara sitting on the rocks on the beach, looking out to sea with a small smile on her face. In one hand she was holding a raven feather, in the other an abalone shell. She looked happy. At peace.

"That's beautiful," Nick said, his voice thick with emotion. "Where do I sign?"

"Anywhere you like," I said, handing him one of my drawing pens.

One by one, everybody signed.

Then we sat and looked at Tara. Some of us cried. Hell, all of us cried.

And then Chad said, "I could kill for a cupcake right now," and at that moment I knew we wouldn't cry forever.

THIRTY-ONE

Alice

I almost didn't go to the reunion Rahim organized.

The truth was, INTRO was the last thing I wanted to think about. I was still waking up every night, my heart racing and my body slick with sweat, thrashing my way out of frantic nightmares. I dreamed about Claire, sweet and smiling, pinning me down and injecting me with insulin or chasing me through the woods with a machete in her hand. The worst dream though—the one that came over and over again—was of me sitting on the beach, on the driftwood log, watching the waves. At first everything seemed normal— peaceful, even—and then I'd notice that the waves were red, and that the water rushing over the gray stones of the beach was actually blood, rushing higher and higher until it was churning thick and warm around my bare feet.

On the days after that dream, I didn't even want to get out of bed.

It was Imogen who persuaded me to go to the reunion. "It's been three months, and you're still kind of a mess. Your whole let's-pretend-it-never-happened strategy isn't working so well," she pointed out.

I couldn't really argue with that.

And now that I was at Rahim's, sitting on his big L-shaped couch between Imogen and Caleb, I was glad to be there.

After we'd all signed Caleb's portrait of Tara, Rahim called for our attention. He laced his fingers together and gazed down at them for a moment. "I want to apologize to you all," he said. "I only graduated a year ago, you know? I've always wanted to work with teens, and I was pretty thrilled to get the job with INTRO. And I...well, obviously, I had no idea. Still, I'm so sorry."

"It's not like you could have known," Nick said. "Claire seemed all right."

"Yes," Rahim said. "I mean, I've taken courses in psychopathology, but I never suspected anything. Maybe I should have." He cleared his throat. "Anyway, you guys saved my life. If you find yourself thinking about INTRO in the middle of the night, try to remember that. You were in a horrific situation, but you coped with it. You showed yourselves to be strong, resourceful and courageous. You should feel good about that."

"I always thought I wanted to be a cop," I blurted out. "A detective. But now...well, it's the last thing I want to do."

"Understandable," Rahim said. "Do you have other ideas?"

My eyes met his. "Law maybe," I told him.

"I could see that," he said. "What about you, Imogen?"

"I'm still clean," she said. "I haven't used since before INTRO."

"That's impressive. Especially after what you've been through. How do you think you managed not to fall back on that as a way of coping?"

She shook her head. "I don't know. But I'm not hanging out with the same people…"

"She's busy with Alice," Chad said.

I waited for his usual snigger, but it never came.

"Well, congratulations to all of you," Rahim said. "I'm so impressed with your strength and resilience, and I'm truly honored to have walked with you on your journey."

It was funny—the way Rahim talked was as goofy as ever, but no one rolled their eyes now. Because those goofy things he said? We all knew he meant every word.

"I've been thinking," Imogen said. "I told Alice this when we were still on the island—about maybe going into counseling. I want to…well, help people. Like you, Rahim."

Rahim blinked a few times and gave her a funny little bow. Then he nodded to himself a few times, like he was collecting his thoughts. "Remember that ceremony we had on the island? With the paper boats?"

I pictured the stiff white paper, the sharp folds. "I wrote *GROUP THERAPY SUCKS*," I admitted.

"Alice!" Imogen gave me a shove.

Rahim laughed.

"Sorry," I said. And then suddenly I was flooded with memories. I could see the tiny boats disappearing in the waves, feel the cold rain on my skin as we left the beach. I could see Tara standing there in the water, jeans rolled up, her back to us all.

"I thought we could do it again," Rahim said. He nodded at Caleb's sketch on the mantel. "For Tara. To say goodbye. To let her go."

My eyes followed his, and I gazed at the portrait. "I'm in."

"Me too," Imogen said. As everyone murmured their agreement, Rahim passed around a stack of white paper and a little ceramic pot full of pens and pencils.

I wanted to write something for Tara, but I didn't know what to say. So in the end I just wrote *Goodbye*.

English Bay was only a few blocks from Rahim's apartment, a short walk. It was a cool, breezy evening, the sun hanging low over the horizon. The sky was striped with color—clear blue fading to orange and pink and gold, with long streaks of backlit cloud.

Imogen and I held hands as we walked along the waterfront. Sometimes I couldn't believe we'd met—that in the middle of all this awfulness, I'd found someone like her.

"How about right here?" Rahim said, pointing.

Boats in our hands, we stepped off the paved path and walked across the sand to the water. There were people sitting on the beach, reading, eating picnic suppers, watching the sunset. Enjoying the late-summer weather.

We must have looked funny—seven of us, sticking tightly together and clutching paper boats—but no one seemed to pay us any attention.

I kicked off my sandals, let go of Imogen's hand and waded into the cold water. The tide was ebbing, and the waves gently lapped at the shore. I bent and lowered my boat. All around me the others did the same.

We stood there silently, watching our boats bob up and down in the water.

After a few minutes I felt a hand on my shoulder and turned to see Caleb smiling down at me from his absurd height. "You okay?" he asked.

"Yeah," I said, surprised by his concern. I wrapped my arms around myself and shivered. "Other than the fact I'm freezing to death."

Caleb shrugged off his hoodie and handed it to me. "Here."

I hesitated—it was such a *guy* thing to do—and Caleb rolled his eyes. "Don't be stupid, Alice. You're cold; I'm not. Okay?"

"Like you'd wear my jacket if you were cold," I said, putting on the hoodie. It came down to my knees, and my hands were lost somewhere way up in the sleeves.

"I would," he said solemnly.

And we both burst out laughing at the image.

"What's the joke?" Imogen asked.

I grinned at her. "Hey. Nothing. Just..." I waggled my long sleeves. "I was cold."

"Yeah, me too. Jason suggested going somewhere for a round of hot chocolate or something. You want to?"

I nodded. "You in, Caleb?"

"Yeah, I'm in."

Imogen grabbed the end of one of my dangling sleeves and Caleb took the other, and we all left the beach together.

ACKNOWLEDGMENTS

This book was a great deal of fun to write. Thanks to Agatha Christie and all the other mystery writers whose novels we devoured as kids. Thanks to Kit Pearson and Kath Farris for letting us stay in their Mayne Island cottage to write the final chapters. Alex Van Tol, Cheryl May and Ilse and Giles Stevenson all read early versions and gave us valuable feedback. Barbara Pulling was our fantastic editor, and her insights were much appreciated. And as always, thanks to the wonderful Orca pod.

Sarah N. Harvey writes for both children and young adults. Some of her books have been translated into Korean, French, German and Slovenian. She lives in Victoria, British Columbia, where she works as a children's book editor. For more information, visit www.sarahnharvey.com.

Robin Stevenson is the author of twenty books for kids and teens. Her novels include *The World Without Us* and *The Summer We Saved the Bees*, as well as the Silver Birch Award winner *Record Breaker* and the Governor General's Award finalist *A Thousand Shades of Blue*. She lives in Victoria, British Columbia. For more information, visit www.robinstevenson.com.

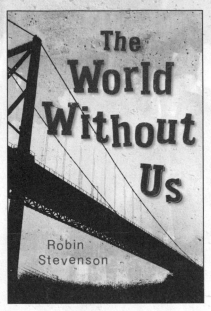